Achilles smiled as Valentina settled herself across the coffee table from him, with a certain inbred grace that whispered of palaces and comportment classes and a lifetime of genteel manners.

Because she thought she was tricking him.

Which meant he could trick her instead. A prospect his body responded to with great enthusiasm as he studied her, this woman who looked like an underling that a man in his position could never have touched out of ethical considerations—but wasn't.

She wasn't his employee. He didn't pay her salary and she wasn't bound to obey him in anything if she didn't feel like it.

But she had no idea that he knew that.

Achilles almost felt sorry for her. Almost.

Caitlin Crews

THE BILLIONAIRE'S SECRET PRINCESS

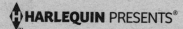

Recycling programs
for this product may
not exist in your area.

ISBN-13: 978-0-373-06082-5

The Billionaire's Secret Princess

First North American Publication 2017

Copyright © 2017 by Caitlin Crews

Printed in U.S.A.

USA TODAY bestselling and RITA® Award—nominated author **Caitlin Crews** loves writing romance. She teaches her favorite romance novels in creative writing classes at places like UCLA Extension's prestigious Writers' Program, where she finally gets to utilize the MA and PhD in English literature she received from the University of York in England. She currently lives in California, with her very own hero and too many pets. Visit her at caitlincrews.com.

Books by Caitlin Crews

Harlequin Presents

Castelli's Virgin Widow
At the Count's Bidding

Scandalous Royal Brides

The Prince's Nine-Month Scandal

Wedlocked!

Bride by Royal Decree
Expecting a Royal Scandal

One Night With Consequences

The Guardian's Virgin Ward

The Billionaire's Legacy

The Return of the Di Sione Wife

Secret Heirs of Billionaires

Unwrapping the Castelli Secret

Scandalous Sheikh Brides

Protecting the Desert Heir
Traded to the Desert Sheikh

The Chatsfield

Greek's Last Redemption

Visit the Author Profile page at Harlequin.com for more titles.

To all the secret princesses cruelly stuck working in horrible offices: as long as you know the truth, that's what matters.

CHAPTER ONE

ACHILLES CASILIERIS REQUIRED PERFECTION.

In himself, certainly. He prided himself on it, knowing all too well how easy it was to fall far, far short. And in his employees, absolutely—or they would quickly find themselves on the other side of their non-compete agreements with indelible black marks against their names.

He did not play around. He had built everything he had from nothing, step by painstaking step, and he hadn't succeeded the way he had—building the recession-proof Casilieris Company and making his first million by the age of twenty-five, then expanding both his business and his personal fortune into the billions—by accepting anything less than 100 percent perfection in all things. Always.

Achilles was tough, tyrannical when necessary, and refused to accept what one short-lived personal assistant had foolishly called "human limitations" to his face.

He was a man who knew the monster in himself. He'd seen its face in his own mirror. He did not allow for "human limitations."

Natalie Monette was his current executive assistant and had held the position for a record five years because she had never once asserted that she was human as some kind of excuse. In point of fact, Achilles thought of her as a remarkably efficient robot—the highest praise he could think to bestow on anyone, as it removed the possibility of human error from the equation.

Achilles had no patience for human error.

Which was why his assistant's behavior on this flight today was so alarming.

The day had started out normally enough. When Achilles had risen at his usual early hour, it had been to find Natalie already hard at work in the study of his Belgravia town house. She'd set up a few calls to his associates in France, outlined his schedule for the day and his upcoming meetings in New York. They'd swung by his corporate offices in the City, where Achilles had handled a fire he thought she should have put out before he'd learned of it, but then she'd accompanied him in his car to the private airfield he preferred without appearing the least bit bothered that he'd dressed her down for her failure. And why should she be bothered? She knew he expected perfection and had failed to deliver it. Besides, Natalie was never bothered. She'd acquitted herself with her usual cool competence and attitude-free demeanor, the way she always did or she never would have lasted five minutes with him. Much less five years.

And then she'd gone into the bathroom at the airfield, stayed in there long enough that he'd had to go find her himself, and come out changed.

Achilles couldn't put his finger on *how* she'd changed, only that she had.

She still looked the part of the closest assistant to a man as feared and lauded as Achilles had been for years now. She looked like his public face the way she always did. He appreciated that and always had. It wasn't enough that she was capable of handling the complications of his personal and company business without breaking a sweat, that she never seemed to sleep, that she could protect him from the intrusive paparazzi and hold off his equally demanding board members in the same breath—it was necessary that she also look like the sort of woman who belonged in his exalted orbit for the rare occasions when he needed to escort someone to this or that function and couldn't trouble himself to expend the modicum of charm necessary to squire one of his mistresses. Today she wore one of her usual outfits, a pencil skirt and soft blouse and a feminine sort of sweater that wrapped around her torso and was no different from any other outfit she'd worn a million times before.

Natalie dressed to disappear in plain sight. But for some reason, she caught his eye this odd afternoon. He couldn't quite figure it out. It was as if he had never seen her before. It was as if she'd gone into the bathroom in the airport lounge and come out a completely different person.

Achilles sat back in his remarkably comfortable leather chair on the jet and watched her as she took her seat opposite him. Did he imagine that she hesitated? Was he making up the strange look he'd seen in her eyes before she sat down? Almost as if she was looking for clues instead of taking her seat as she always did?

"What took you so long in that bathroom?" he asked, not bothering to keep his tone particularly polite. "I should not have to chase down my own assistant, surely."

Natalie blinked. He didn't know why the green of her eyes behind the glasses he knew she didn't need for sight seemed…too bright, somehow. Or brighter, anyway, than they'd been before. In fact, now that he thought about it, everything about her was brighter. And he couldn't understand how anyone could walk into a regular lavatory and come out…gleaming.

"I apologize," she said quietly. Simply. And there was something about her voice then. It was almost… musical.

It occurred to Achilles that he had certainly never thought of Natalie's voice as anything approaching *musical* before. It had always been a voice, pure and simple. And she had certainly never *gleamed*.

And that, he thought with impatience, was one of the reasons that he had prized Natalie so much for all these years. Because he had never, ever noticed her as anything but his executive assistant, who was reasonably attractive because it was good business to give his Neanderthal cronies something worth gazing at while they were trying to ignore Achilles's dominance. But there was a difference between noting that a woman was attractive and *being attracted to* that woman. Achilles would not have hired Natalie if he'd been attracted to her. He never had been. Not ever.

But to his utter astonishment that was what seemed to be happening. Right here. Right now. His body was sending him unambiguous signals. He wasn't simply *attracted* to his assistant. What he felt roll in him as she crossed her legs at the ankle and smiled at him was far more than *attraction*.

It was need.

Blinding and impossible and incredibly, astonishingly inconvenient.

Achilles Casilieris did not do inconvenience, and he was violently opposed to *need*. It had been beaten into him as an unwanted child that it was the height of foolishness to want something he couldn't have. That meant he'd dedicated his adult life to never allowing himself to need anything at all when he could buy whatever took his fancy, and he hadn't.

And yet there was no denying that dark thread that wound in him, pulling tight and succeeding in surprising him—something else that happened very, very rarely.

Achilles knew the shadows that lived in him. He had no intention of revisiting them. Ever.

Whatever his assistant was doing, she needed to stop. Now.

"That is all you wish to say?" He sounded edgy. Dangerous. He didn't like that, either.

But Natalie hardly seemed to notice. "If you would like me to expand on my apology, Mr. Casilieris, you need only tell me how."

He thought there was a subtle rebuke in that, no matter how softly she'd said it, and that, too, was new. And unacceptable no matter how prettily she'd voiced it.

Her copper-colored hair gleamed. Her skin glowed as she moved her hands in her lap, which struck him as odd, because Natalie never sat there with her hands folded in her lap like some kind of diffident Catholic schoolgirl. She was always in motion, because she was always working. But tonight, Natalie appeared to be sitting there like some kind of regal Madonna, hands folded in her lap, long, silky legs crossed at the ankles, and an inappropriately serene smile on her face.

If it wasn't impossible, he would have thought that she really was someone else entirely. Because she looked exactly the same save for all that gold that seemed to wrap itself around her and him, too, making him unduly fascinated with the pulse he could see beating at her throat—except he'd never, ever noticed her that way before.

Achilles did not have time for this, whatever it was. There was entirely too much going on with his businesses at the moment, like the hotel deal he'd been trying to put together for the better part of the last year that was by no means assured. He hadn't become one of the most feared and fearsome billionaires in the world because he took time off from running his businesses to pretend to care about the personal lives of his employees.

But Natalie wasn't just any employee. She was the one he'd actually come to rely on. The only person he relied on in the world, to be specific.

"Is there anything you need to tell me?" he asked.

He watched her, perhaps too carefully. It was impossible not to notice the way she flushed slightly at that. That was strange, too. He couldn't remember a single instance Natalie had ever flushed in response to anything he'd done. And the truth was he'd done a lot. He didn't hide his flashes of irritation or spend too much time worrying about anyone else's feelings. Why should he? The Casilieris Company was about profit— and it was about Achilles. Who else's feelings should matter? One of the things he'd long prized about his assistant was that she never, ever reacted to anything that he did or said or shouted. She just did her job.

But today Natalie had spots of red, high on her elegant cheekbones, and she'd been sitting across from him for whole minutes now without doing a single thing that could be construed as her job.

Elegant? demanded an incredulous voice inside him. *Cheekbones?*

Since when had Achilles ever noticed anything of the kind? He didn't pay that much attention to the mistresses he took to his bed—which he deigned to do in the first place only after they passed through all the levels of his application process and signed strict confidentiality agreements. And the women who made it through were in no doubt as to why they were there. It was to please him, not render him disoriented enough to be focusing on their bloody *cheekbones*.

"Like what, for example?" She asked the question and then she smiled at him, that curve of her mouth that was suddenly wired to the hardest part of him, and echoed inside him like heat. Heat he didn't want. "I'll be happy to tell you anything you wish to hear, Mr. Casilieris. That is, after all, my job."

"Is that your job?" He smiled, and he doubted it echoed much of anywhere. Or was anything but edgy and a little but harsh. "I had started to doubt that you remembered you had one."

"Because I kept you waiting? That was unusual, it's true."

"You've never done so before. You've never dared." He tilted his head slightly as he gazed at her, not understanding why everything was different when nothing was. He could see that she was exactly the same as she always was, down to that single freckle centered on her left cheekbone that he wasn't even aware he'd noticed before now. "Again, has some tragedy befallen you? Were you hit over the head?" He did nothing to hide the warning or the menace in his voice. "You do not appear to be yourself."

But if he thought he'd managed to discomfit her, he saw in the next moment that was not to be. The flush faded from her porcelain cheeks, and all she did was smile at him again. With that maddeningly enigmatic curve of her lips.

Lips, he noticed with entirely too much of his body, that were remarkably lush.

This was insupportable.

"I am desolated to disappoint you," she murmured as the plane began to move, bumping gently along the tarmac. "But there was no tragedy." Something glinted in her green gaze, though her smile never dimmed.

"Though I must confess in the spirit of full disclosure that I was thinking of quitting."

Achilles only watched her idly, as if she hadn't just said that. Because she couldn't possibly have just said that.

"I beg your pardon," he said after a moment passed and there was still that spike of something dark and furious in his chest. "I must have misheard you. You do not mean that you plan to quit this job. That you wish to leave *me*."

It was not lost on him that he'd phrased that in a way that should have horrified him. Maybe it would at some point. But today what slapped at him was that his assistant spoke of quitting without a single hint of anything like uncertainty on her face.

And he found he couldn't tolerate that.

"I'm considering it," she said. Still smiling. Unaware of her own danger or the dark thing rolling in him, reminding him of how easy it was to wake that monster that slept in him. How disastrously easy.

But Achilles laughed then, understanding finally catching up with him. "If this is an attempt to wrangle more money out of me, Miss Monette, I cannot say that I admire the strategy. You're perfectly well compensated as is. Overcompensated, one might say."

"Might one? Perhaps." She looked unmoved. "Then again, perhaps your rivals have noticed exactly how much you rely on me. Perhaps I've decided that I want more than being at the beck and call of a billionaire. Much less standing in as your favorite bit of target practice."

"It cannot possibly have bothered you that I lost my temper earlier."

Her smile was bland. "If you say it cannot, then I'm sure you must be right."

"I lose my temper all the time. It's never bothered you before. It's part of your job to not be bothered, in point of fact."

"I'm certain that's it." Her enigmatic smile seemed to deepen. "I must be the one who isn't any good at her job."

He had the most insane notion then. It was something about the cool challenge in her gaze, as if they were equals. As if she had every right to call him on whatever she pleased. He had no idea why he wanted to reach across the little space between their chairs and put his hands on her. Test her skin to see if it was as soft as it looked. Taste that lush mouth—

What the hell was happening to him?

Achilles shook his head, as much to clear it as anything else. "If this is your version of a negotiation, you should rethink your approach. You know perfectly well that there's entirely too much going on right now."

"Some might think that this is the perfect time, then, to talk about things like compensation and temper tantrums," Natalie replied, her voice as even and unbothered as ever. There was no reason that should make him grit his teeth. "After all, when one is expected to work twenty-two hours a day and is shouted at for her trouble, one's thoughts automatically turn to what one lacks. It's human nature."

"You lack nothing. You have no time to spend the

money I pay you because you're too busy traveling the world—which I also pay for."

"If only I had more than two hours a day to enjoy these piles of money."

"People would kill for the opportunity to spend even five minutes in my presence," he reminded her. "Or have you forgotten who I am?"

"Come now." She shook her head at him, and he had the astonishing sense that she was trying to chastise him. *Him.* "It would not kill you to be more polite, would it?"

Polite.

His own assistant had just lectured him on his manners.

To say that he was reeling hardly began to scratch the surface of Achilles's reaction.

But then she smiled, and that reaction got more complicated. "I got on the plane anyway. I decided not to quit today." Achilles could not possibly have missed her emphasis on that final word. "You're welcome."

And something began to build inside him at that. Something huge, dark, almost overwhelming. He was very much afraid it was rage.

But that, he refused. No matter what. Achilles left his demons behind him a long time ago, and he wasn't going back. He refused.

"If you would like to leave, Miss Monette, I will not stop you," he assured her coldly. "I cannot begin to imagine what has led you to imagine I would try. I do not beg. I could fill your position with a snap of my fingers. I might yet, simply because this conversation is intolerable."

The assistant he'd thought he knew would have swallowed hard at that, then looked away. She would have smoothed her hands over her skirt and apologized as she did it. She had riled him only a few times over the years, and she'd talked her way out of it in exactly that way. He gazed at her expectantly.

But today, Natalie only sat there with distractingly perfect posture and gazed back at him with a certain serene confidence that made him want to…mess her up. Get his hands in that unremarkable ponytail and feel the texture of all that gleaming copper. Or beneath her snowy-white blouse. Or better yet, up beneath that skirt of hers.

He was so furious he wasn't nearly as appalled at himself as he should have been.

"I think we both know perfectly well that while you could snap your fingers and summon crowds of candidates for my position, you'd have a very hard time filling it to your satisfaction," she said with a certainty that…gnawed at him. "Perhaps we could dispense with the threats. You need me."

He would sooner have her leap forward and plunge a knife into his chest.

"I need no one," he rasped out. "And nothing."

His suddenly mysterious assistant only inclined her head, which he realized was no response at all. As if she was merely patronizing him—a notion that made every muscle in his body clench tight.

"You should worry less about your replacement and

more about your job," Achilles gritted out. "I have no idea what makes you think you can speak to me with such disrespect."

"It is not disrespectful to speak frankly, surely," she said. Her expression didn't change, but her green gaze was grave—very much, he thought with dawning incredulity, as if she'd expected better of him.

Achilles could only stare back at her in arrogant astonishment. Was he now to suffer the indignity of being judged by his own assistant? And why was it she seemed wholly uncowed by his amazement?

"Unless you plan to utilize a parachute, it would appear you are stuck right here in your distasteful position for the next few hours," Achilles growled at her when he thought he could speak without shouting. Shouting was too easy. And obscured his actual feelings. "I'd suggest you use the time to rethink your current attitude."

He didn't care for the brilliant smile she aimed at him then, as if she was attempting to encourage him with it. *Him*. He particularly didn't like the way it seemed too bright, as if it was lighting him up from the inside out.

"What a kind offer, Mr. Casilieris," she said in that self-possessed voice of hers that was driving him mad. "I will keep it in mind."

The plane took off then, somersaulting into the London sky. Achilles let gravity press him back against the seat and considered the evidence before him. He had worked with this woman for five years, and she had never spoken to him like that before. Ever. He hardly knew what to make of it.

But then, there was a great deal he didn't know what to do with, suddenly. The way his heart pounded against his ribs as if he was in a real temper, when he was not the sort of man who lost control. Of his temper or anything else. He expected nothing less than perfection from himself, first and foremost. And temper made him think of those long-ago days of his youth, and his stepfather's hovel of a house, victim to every stray whim and temper and fist until he'd given himself over to all that rage and fury inside him and become little better than an animal himself—

Why was he allowing himself to think of such things? His youth was off-limits, even in his own head. What the hell was *happening*?

Achilles didn't like that Natalie affected him. But what made him suspicious was that she'd never affected him before. He'd approved when she started to wear those glasses and put her hair up, to make herself less of a target for the less scrupulous men he dealt with who thought they could get to him through expressing their interest in her. But he hadn't needed her to downplay her looks because *he* was entranced by her. He hadn't been.

So what had changed today?

What had emboldened her and, worse, allowed her to get under his skin?

He kept circling back to that bathroom in the airport and the fact she'd walked out of it a different person from the one who'd walked in.

Of course, she wasn't a *different person*. Did he imagine the real Natalie had suffered a body snatching? Did he imagine there was some elaborate hoax afoot?

The idea was absurd. But he couldn't seem to get past it. The plane hit its cruising altitude, and he moved from his chair to the leather couch that took pride of place in the center of the cabin that was set up like one of his high-end hotel rooms. He sat back with his laptop and pretended to be looking through his email when he was watching Natalie instead. Looking for clues.

She wasn't moving around the plane with her usual focus and energy. He thought she seemed tentative. Uncertain—and this despite the fact she seemed to walk taller than before. As if she'd changed her very posture in that bathroom. But who did something like that?

A different person would have different posture.

It was crazy. He knew that. And Achilles knew further that he always went a little too intense when he was closing a deal, so it shouldn't have surprised him that he was willing to consider the insane option today. Part of being the sort of unexpected, out-of-the-box thinker he'd always been was allowing his mad little flights of fancy. He never knew where they might lead.

He indulged himself as Natalie sat and started to look through her own bag as if she'd never seen it before. He pulled up the picture of her he kept in his files for security purposes and did an image search on it, because why not.

Achilles was prepared to discover a few photos of random celebrities she resembled, maybe. And then he'd have to face the fact that his favorite assistant might have gone off the deep end. She was right that replacing her would be hard—but it wouldn't be impossible. He hadn't overestimated his appeal—and that of his wildly successful company—to pretty much anyone and everyone. He was swamped with applicants daily, and he didn't even have an open position.

But then none of that mattered because his image search hit gold.

There were pages and pages of pictures. All of his assistant—except it wasn't her. He knew it from the exquisitely bespoke gowns she wore. He knew it from the jewels that flowed around her neck and covered her hands, drawing attention to things like the perfect manicure she had today—when the Natalie he knew almost never had time to care for her nails like that. And every picture he clicked on identified the woman in them not as Natalie Monette, assistant to Achilles Casilieris, but Her Royal Highness, Princess Valentina of Murin.

Achilles didn't have much use for royals, or really anyone with inherited wealth, when he'd had to go to so much trouble to amass his own. He'd never been to the tiny Mediterranean kingdom of Murin, mostly because he didn't have a yacht to dock there during a sparkling summer of endless lounging and, further, didn't need to take advantage of the country's famously friendly approach to taxes. But he recognized King Geoffrey of Murin on sight, and he certainly recognized the Murinese royal family's coat of arms.

It had been splashed all over the private jet he'd seen on the same tarmac as his back in London.

There was madness, Achilles thought then, and then there was a con job that no one would ever suspect—because who could imagine that the person standing in front of them, looking like someone they already knew, was actually someone else?

If he wasn't mistaken—and he knew he wasn't, because there were too many things about his assistant today that didn't make sense, and Achilles was no great believer in coincidence—Princess Valentina of Murin was trying to run a con.

On him.

Which meant a great many things. First, that his actual assistant was very likely pretending to be the princess somewhere, leaving him and her job in the hands of someone she had to know would fail to live up to Achilles's high standards. That suggested that second, she really wasn't all that happy in her position, as this princess had dared to throw in his face in a way he doubted Natalie ever would have. But it also suggested that third, Natalie had effectively given her notice.

Achilles didn't like any of that. At all. But the fourth thing that occurred to him was that clearly, neither this princess nor his missing assistant expected their little switch to be noticed. Natalie, who should have known better, must honestly have believed that he wouldn't notice an imposter in her place. Or she hadn't cared much if he did.

That was enraging, on some level. Insulting.

But Achilles smiled as Valentina settled herself across the coffee table from him, with a certain inbred grace that whispered of palaces and comportment classes and a lifetime of genteel manners.

Because she thought she was tricking him.

Which meant he could trick her instead. A prospect his body responded to with great enthusiasm as he studied her, this woman who looked like an underling whom a man in his position could never have touched out of ethical considerations—but wasn't.

She wasn't his employee. He didn't pay her salary, and she wasn't bound to obey him in anything if she didn't feel like it.

But she had no idea that he knew that.

Achilles almost felt sorry for her. Almost.

"Let's get started," he murmured, as if they'd exchanged no harsh words. He watched confusion move over her face in a blink, then disappear, because she was a royal princess and she was used to concealing her reactions. He planned to have fun with that. The possibilities were endless, and seemed to roll through him like heat. "We have so much work to do, Miss Monette. I hardly know where to begin."

CHAPTER TWO

BY THE TIME they landed in New York, Princess Valentina of Murin was second-guessing her spontaneous, impulsive decision to switch places with the perfect stranger she'd found wearing her face in the airport lounge.

Achilles Casilieris could make anyone second-guess anything, she suspected.

"You do not appear to be paying attention," he said silkily from beside her, as if he knew exactly what she was thinking. And who she was. And every dream she'd ever had since she was a girl—that was how disconcerting this man was, even lounging there beside her in the back of a luxury car doing nothing more alarming than *sitting*.

"I am hanging on your every word," she assured him as calmly as she could, and then she repeated his last three sentences back to him.

But she had no idea what he was talking about. Repeating conversations she wasn't really listening to was a skill she'd learned in the palace a long, long time ago. It came in handy at many a royal gathering. And in many longwinded lectures from her father and his staff.

You have thrown yourself into deep, deep water, she told herself now, as if that wasn't entirely too apparent already. As if it hadn't already occurred to her that she'd better learn how to swim, and fast.

Achilles Casilieris was a problem.

Valentina knew powerful men. Men who ruled countries. Men who came from centuries upon centuries of power and consequence and wielded it with the offhanded superiority of those who had never imagined *not* ruling all they surveyed.

But Achilles was in an entirely different league.

He took over the whole of the backseat of the car that had waited for them on the tarmac in the bright and sunny afternoon, looking roomy and spacious from the outside. He'd insisted she sit next to him on the plush backseat that should have been more than able to fit two people with room to spare. And yet Valentina felt crowded, as if he was pressing up against her when he wasn't. Achilles wasn't touching her, but still, she was entirely too *aware* of him.

He took up all the air. He'd done it on his plane, too.

She had the hectic notion, connected to that knot beneath her breastbone that was preventing her from taking anything like a deep breath, that it wasn't the enclosed space that was the issue. That he would have this same effect anywhere. All that brooding ruthlessness he didn't bother to contain—or maybe he couldn't contain even if he'd wanted to—seemed to hum around him like a kind of force field that both repelled and compelled at once.

If she was honest, the little glimpse she'd had of

him in the airport had been the same—she'd just ignored it.

Valentina had been too busy racing into the lounge so she could have a few precious seconds alone. No staff. No guards. No cameras. Just her perched on the top of a closed toilet seat, shut away from the world, breathing. Letting her face do what it liked. Thinking of absolutely nothing. Not her duty. Not her father's expectations.

Certainly not her bloodless engagement to Prince Rodolfo of Tissely, a man she'd tuned out within moments of their first meeting. Or their impending wedding in two months' time, which she could feel bearing down on her like a thick hand around her throat every time she let herself think about it. It wasn't that she didn't *want* to do her duty and marry the Crown Prince of Tissely. She'd been promised in marriage to her father's allies since the day she was born. It was that she'd never given a great deal of thought to what it was she wanted, because *want* had never been an option available to her.

And it had suddenly occurred to her at her latest wedding dress fitting there in London that she was running out of time.

Soon she would be married to a man in what was really more of a corporate merger of two great European brands, the houses of Tissely and Murin. She'd be expected to produce the necessary heirs to continue the line. She would take her place in the great sweep of her family's storied history, unite two ancient kingdoms, and in so doing fulfill her purpose in life. The end.

The end, she'd thought in that bathroom stall, high-end and luxurious but still, a bathroom stall. *My life fulfilled at twenty-seven.*

Valentina was a woman who'd been given everything, including a healthy understanding of how lucky she was. She didn't often indulge herself with thoughts of what was and wasn't fair when there was no doubt she was among the most fortunate people alive.

But the thing was, it still didn't seem fair. No matter how hard she tried not to think about it that way.

She would do what she had to do, of course. She always had and always would, but for that single moment, locked away in a bathroom stall where no one could see her and no one would ever know, she basked in the sheer, dizzying unfairness of it all.

Then she'd pulled herself together, stepped out and had been prepared to march onto her plane and head back to the life that had been plotted out for her since the day she arrived on the planet.

Only to find her twin standing at the sinks.

Her identical twin—though that was, of course, impossible.

"What is this?" the other woman had asked when they'd faced each other, looking something close to scared. Or unnerved, anyway. "How…?"

Valentina had been fascinated. She'd been unable to keep herself from studying this woman who appeared to be wearing her body as well as her face. She was dressed in a sleek pencil skirt and low heels, which showed legs that Valentina recognized all too well, having last seen them in her own mirror. "I'm Valentina."

"Natalie."

She'd repeated that name in her head like it was a magic spell. She didn't know why she felt as if it was.

But then, running into her double in a London bathroom seemed something close enough to magic to count. Right then when she'd been indulging her self-pity about the unchangeable course of her own life, the universe had presented her with a glimpse of what else could be. If she was someone else.

An identical someone else.

They had the same face. The same legs, as she'd already noted. The same coppery hair that her double wore up in a serviceable ponytail and the same nose Valentina could trace directly to her maternal grandmother. What were the chances, she'd wondered then, that they *weren't* related?

And didn't that raise all kinds of interesting questions?

"You're that princess," Natalie had said, a bit haltingly.

But if Valentina was a princess, and if they were related as they surely had to be...

"I suspect you might be, too," she'd said gently.

"We can't possibly be related. I'm a glorified secretary who never really had a home. You're a royal princess. Presumably your lineage dates back to the Roman Conquest."

"Give or take a few centuries." Valentina tried to imagine having a job like that. Or any job. A secretary, glorified or otherwise, who reported to work for someone else and actually *did things* with her time that weren't directly related to being a symbol. She couldn't really wrap her head around it, or being effectively without a home, either, having been a part of Murin since her birth. As much Murin as its beaches and hills, its monuments and its palace. She might as well have been a park. "Depending which branch of the family you mean, of course."

"I was under the impression that people with lineages that could lead to thrones and crown jewels tended to keep better track of their members," Natalie had said, her tone just dry enough to make Valentina decide that given the right circumstances—meaning anywhere that wasn't a toilet—she'd rather like her doppelganger.

And she knew what the other woman had been asking.

"Conspiracy theorists claim my mother was killed and her death hushed up. Senior palace officials have assured me my whole life that no, she merely left to preserve her mental health, and is rumored to be in residence in a hospital devoted to such things somewhere. All I know is that I haven't seen her since shortly after I was born. According to my father, she preferred anonymity to the joys of motherhood."

And she waited for Natalie to give her an explanation in turn. To laugh, perhaps, and then tell her that she'd been raised by two perfectly normal parents in a happily normal somewhere else, filled with golden retrievers and school buses and pumpkin-spiced coffee drinks and whatever else normal people took for granted that Valentina only read about.

But instead, this woman wearing Valentina's face had looked stricken. "I've never met my father," she'd whispered. "My mother's always told me she has no idea who he was. And she bounces from one affair to the next pretty quickly, so I came to terms with the fact it was possible she really, truly didn't know."

And Valentina had laughed, because what else could she do? She'd spent her whole life wishing she'd had more of a family than her chilly father. Oh, she loved him, she did, but he was so excruciatingly proper. So worried about appearances. His version of a hug was a well-meaning critique on her latest public appearance. Love to her father was maintaining and bolstering the family's reputation across the ages. She'd always wanted a sister to share in the bolstering. A brother. A mother. *Someone.*

But she hadn't had anyone. And now she had a stranger who looked just like her.

"My father is many things," she'd told Natalie. It was too soon to say *our father.* And who knew? Maybe they were cousins. Or maybe this was a fluke. No matter that little jolt of recognition inside her, as if she'd been meant to know this woman. As if this was a reunion. "Including His Royal Majesty, King Geoffrey of Murin. What he is not now, nor has ever been, I imagine, is forgettable."

Natalie had shaken her head. "You underestimate my mother's commitment to amnesia. She's made it a life choice instead of a malady. On some level I admire it."

"My mother was the noblewoman Frederica de

Burgh, from a very old Murinese family." Valentina watched Natalie closely as she spoke, looking for any hint of…anything, really, in her gaze. "Promised to my father at birth, raised by nuns and kept deliberately sheltered, and then widely held to be unequal to the task of becoming queen. Mentally. But that's the story they would tell, isn't it, to explain why she disappeared? What's your mother's name?"

Natalie sighed and swung her shoulder bag onto the counter. Valentina had the impression that she'd really, truly wanted not to answer. But she had. "She calls herself Erica."

And there it was. Valentina supposed it could be a coincidence that *Erica* was a shortened form of *Frederica*. But how many coincidences were likely when they resulted in two women who'd never met—who never should have met—who happened to be mirror images?

If there was something in her that turned over at the notion that her mother had, in fact, had a maternal impulse after all—just not for Valentina—well, this wasn't the time to think about that. It might never be the time to think about that. She'd spent twenty-seven years trying her best not to think about that.

She changed the subject before she lost her composure completely and started asking questions she knew she shouldn't.

"I saw Achilles Casilieris, out there in the lounge," she'd said instead. The notorious billionaire had been there on her way in, brooding in a corner of the lounge and scowling at the paper he'd been reading. "He looks even more fearsome in person. You can almost *see* all that brash command and dizzying wealth ooze from his pores, can't you?"

"He's my boss," Natalie had said, sounding amused—if rather darkly. "If he was really oozing anything, anywhere, it would be my job to provide first aid until actual medical personnel could come handle it. At which point he would bite my head off for wasting his precious time by not curing him instantly."

Valentina had been flooded with a rash of follow-up questions. Was the biting off of heads normal? Was it fun to work for a man who sounded half-feral? Most important, did Natalie like her life or merely suffer through it?

But then her mobile started buzzing in her clutch. She'd forgotten about ferocious billionaires and thought about things she knew too much about, like the daredevil prince she was bound to marry soon, instead, because their fathers had agreed regardless of whether either one of them liked it. She'd checked the mobile's display to be sure, but wasn't surprised to find she'd guessed correctly. Lucky her, she'd had another meeting with her husband-to-be in Murin that very afternoon. She'd expected it to go the way all their meetings so far had gone. Prince Rodolfo, beloved the world over for his good looks and devil-may-care attitude, would talk. She would listen without really listening. She'd long since concluded that foretold a very happy royal marriage.

"My fiancé," she'd explained, meeting Natalie's gaze again. "Or his chief of staff, to be more precise."

"Congratulations," Natalie murmured.

"Thank you, I'm very lucky." Valentina's mouth curved, though her tone was far more dry than Natalie's had been. "Everyone says so. Prince Rodolfo is objectively attractive. Not all princes can make that claim, but the tabloids have exulted over his abs since he was a teenager. Just as they have salivated over his impressive dating history, which has involved a selection of models and actresses from at least four continents and did not cease in any noticeable way upon our engagement last fall."

"Your Prince Charming sounds…charming," Natalie had said.

Valentina raised one shoulder, then dropped it. "His theory is that he remains free until our marriage, and then will be free once again following the necessary birth of his heir. More discreetly, I can only hope. Meanwhile, I am beside myself with joy that I must take my place at his side in two short months. Of course."

Natalie had laughed, and the sound had made Valentina's stomach flip. Because it sounded like her. It sounded exactly like her.

"It's going to be a terrific couple of months all around, then," her mirror image was saying. "Mr. Casilieris is in rare form. He's putting together a particularly dramatic deal and it's not going his way and he… isn't used to that. So that's me working twenty-two-hour days instead of my usual twenty for the foreseeable future, which is even more fun when he's cranky and snarling."

"It can't possibly be worse than having to smile politely while your future husband lectures you about the absurd expectation of fidelity in what is essentially an arranged marriage for hours on end. The absurdity is that *he* might be expected to curb his impulses for a year or so, in case you wondered. The expectations for *me* apparently involve quietly and chastely finding fulfillment in philanthropic works, like his sainted absentee mother, who everyone knows manufactured a supposed health crisis so she could live out her days in peaceful seclusion. It's easy to be philanthropically fulfilled while living in isolation in Bavaria."

Natalie had smiled. "Try biting your tongue while your famously short-tempered boss rages at you for no reason, for the hundredth time in an hour, because he pays you to stand there and take it without wilting or crying or selling whingeing stories about him to the press."

Valentina had returned that smile. "Or the hours and hours of grim palace-vetted prewedding press interviews in the company of a pack of advisers who will censor everything I say and inevitably make me sound like a bit of animated treacle, as out of touch with reality as the average overly sweet dessert."

"Speaking of treats, I also have to deal with the board of directors Mr. Casilieris treats like irritating schoolchildren, his packs of furious ex-lovers each with her own vendetta, all his terrified employees who need to be coached through meetings with him and treated for PTSD after, and every last member of his staff in every one of his households, who like me to be the one to ask him the questions they know will set him off on one of his scorch-the-earth rages." Natalie had moved closer then, and lowered her voice. "I was thinking of quitting, to be honest. Today."

"I can't quit, I'm afraid," Valentina had said. Regretfully.

But she'd wished she could. She'd wished she could just…walk away and not have to live up to anyone's expectations. And not have to marry a man whom she barely knew. And not have to resign herself to a version of the same life so many of her ancestors had lived. Maybe that was where the idea had come from. Blood was blood, after all. And this woman clearly shared her blood. What if…?

"I have a better idea," she'd said, and then she'd tossed it out there before she could think better of it. "Let's switch places. For a month, say. Six weeks at the most. Just for a little break."

"That's crazy," Natalie said at once, and she was right. Of course she was right.

"Insane," Valentina had agreed. "But you might find royal protocol exciting! And I've always wanted to do the things everyone else in the world does. Like go to a real job."

"People can't *switch places*." Natalie had frowned. "And certainly not with a princess."

"You could think about whether or not you really want to quit," Valentina pointed out, trying to sweeten the deal. "It would be a lovely holiday for you. Where will Achilles Casilieris be in six weeks' time?"

"He's never gone from London for too long," Natalie had said, as if she was considering it.

Valentina had smiled. "Then in six weeks we'll meet in London. We'll text in the meantime with all the necessary details about our lives, and on the appointed day we'll just meet up and switch back and no one will ever be the wiser. Doesn't that sound like *fun*?"

"It would never work," Natalie had replied. Which wasn't exactly a *no*. "No one will ever believe I'm you."

Valentina waved a hand, encompassing the pair of them. "How would anyone know the difference? I can barely tell myself."

"People will take one look at me and know I'm not you. *You* look like a *princess*."

"You, too, can look like a princess," Valentina assured her. Then smiled. "This princess, anyway. You already do."

"You're elegant. Poised. You've had years of training, presumably. How to be a diplomat. How to be polite in every possible situation. Which fork to use at dinner, for God's sake."

"Achilles Casilieris is one of the wealthiest men alive," Valentina had pointed out. "He dines with as many kings as I do. I suspect that as his personal assistant, Natalie, you have, too. And have likely learned how to navigate the cutlery."

"No one will believe it," Natalie had insisted. But she'd sounded a bit as if she was wavering.

Valentina tugged off the ring on her left hand and placed it down on the counter between them. It made an audible *clink* against the marble surface, as well it should, given it was one of the crown jewels of the kingdom of Tissely.

"Try it on. I dare you. It's an heirloom from Prince Rodolfo's extensive treasury of such items, dating back to the dawn of time, more or less." She smiled. "If it doesn't fit we'll never speak of switching places again."

But the ring had fit her double as if it had been made especially for her.

And after that, switching clothes was easy. Valentina found herself in front of the bathroom mirror, dressed like a billionaire's assistant, when Natalie walked out of the stall behind her in her own shift dress and the heels her favorite shoe designer had made just for her. It was like looking in a mirror, but one that walked and looked unsteady on her feet and was wearing her hair differently.

Valentina couldn't tell if she was disconcerted or excited. Both, maybe.

She'd eyed Natalie. "Will your glasses give me a headache, do you suppose?"

But Natalie had pulled them from her face and handed them over. "They're clear glass. I was getting a little too much attention from some of the men Mr. Casilieris works with, and it annoyed him. I didn't want to lose my job, so I started wearing my hair up and these glasses. It worked like a charm."

"I refuse to believe men are so idiotic."

Natalie had grinned as Valentina took the glasses and slid them onto her nose. "The men we're talking about weren't exactly paying me attention because they found me enthralling. It was a diversionary tactic during negotiations, and yes, you'd be surprised how many men fail to see a woman who looks smart."

She'd freed her hair from its utilitarian ponytail and shook it out, then handed the stretchy elastic to Valentina. It took Valentina a moment to re-create the ponytail on her own head, and then it was done.

And it really was like magic.

"This is crazy," Natalie had whispered.

"We have to switch places now," Valentina said softly, hearing the rough patch in her own voice. "I've always wanted to be…someone else. Someone normal. Just for a little while."

And she'd gotten exactly what she'd wanted, hadn't she?

"I am distressed, Miss Monette, that I cannot manage to secure your attention for more than a moment or two," Achilles said then, slamming Valentina back into this car he dominated so easily when all he was doing was sitting there.

Sitting there, filling up the world without even trying.

He was *devastating*. There was no other possible word that could describe him. His black hair was close-cropped to his head, which only served to highlight his strong, intensely masculine features. She'd had hours on the plane to study him as she'd repeatedly failed to do the things he'd expected of her, and she still couldn't really get her head around why it was that he was so… affecting. He shouldn't have been. Dark hair. Dark eyes that tended toward gold when his temper washed over him, which he'd so far made no attempt to hide. A strong nose that reminded her of ancient statues she'd seen in famous museums. That lean, hard body of his that wasn't made of marble or bronze but seemed to suggest both as he used it so effortlessly. A predator packed into a dark suit that seemed molded to him, whispering suggestions of a lethal warrior when all he was doing was taking phone calls with a five-hundred-thousand-dollar watch on one wrist that he didn't flash about, because he was Achilles Casilieris. He didn't need flash.

Achilles was something else.

It was the power that seemed to emanate from him, even when he was doing nothing but sitting quietly. It was the fierce hit of his intelligence, that brooding, unmistakable cleverness that seemed to wrap around him like a cloud. It was something in the way he looked at her, as if he saw too much and too deeply and no matter that Valentina's unreadable game face was the envy of Europe. Besides all that, there was something untamed about him. Fierce.

Something about him left her breathless. Entirely too close to reeling.

"Do you require a gold star every time you make a statement?" she asked, careful not to look at him. It was too hard to look away. She'd discovered that on the plane ride from London—and he was a lot closer now. So close she was sure she could feel the heat of his body from where she sat. "I'll be certain to make a note to celebrate you more often. Sir."

Valentina didn't know what she was doing. In Natalie's job, certainly, but also with this man in general.

She'd learned one thing about powerful people—particularly men—and it was that they did not enjoy being challenged. Under any circumstances. What made her think Achilles would go against type and magically handle this well?

But she couldn't seem to stop herself.

And the fact that she had never been one to challenge much of anything before hardly signified. Or maybe that was why she felt so unfettered, she thought. Because this wasn't her life. This wasn't her remote father and his endless expectations for the behavior of his only child. This was a strange little bit of role-playing that allowed her to be someone other than Princess Valentina for a moment. A few weeks, that was all. Why not challenge Achilles while she was at it? *Especially* if no one else ever did?

She could feel his gaze on the side of her face, that brooding dark gold, and she braced herself. Then made sure her expression was nothing but serene as she turned to face him.

It didn't matter. There was no minimizing this man. She could feel the hit of him—like a fist—deep in her belly. And then lower.

"Are you certain you were not hit in the head?" Achilles asked, his dark voice faintly rough with the hint of his native Greek. "Perhaps in the bathroom at the airport? I fear that such places can often suffer from slippery floors. Deadly traps for the unwary."

"It was only a bathroom," she replied airily. "It wasn't slippery or otherwise notable in any way."

"Are you sure?" And something in his voice and

his hard gaze prickled into her then. Making her chest feel tighter.

Valentina did not want to talk about the bathroom, much less anything that had happened there. And there was something in his gaze that worried her—but that was insane. He couldn't have any idea that she'd run into her own twin. How could he? Valentina had been unaware that there was the faintest possibility she might have a twin until today.

Which made her think about her father and his many, many lectures about his only child in a new, unfortunate light. But Valentina thrust that aside. That was something to worry about when she was a princess again. That was a problem she could take up when she was back in Murin Castle.

Here, now, she was a secretary. An executive assistant, no more and no less.

"I beg your pardon, Mr. Casilieris." She let her smile deepen and ignored the little hum of…something deep inside her when his gaze seemed to catch fire. "Are you trying to tell me that you need a bathroom? Should I ask the driver to stop the car right here in the middle of the George Washington Bridge?"

She expected him to get angry again. Surely that was what had been going on before, back in London before the plane had taken off. She'd seen temper all over that fierce, hard face of his and gleaming hot in his gaze. More than that, she'd felt it inside her. As if the things he felt echoed within her, winding her into knots. She felt something a whole lot like a chill inch its way down her spine at that notion.

But Achilles only smiled. And that was far more dangerous than merely devastating.

"Miss Monette," he said and shook his head, as if she amused him, when she could see that the thing that moved over that ruthless face of his was far too intense to be simple *amusement*. "I had no idea that beneath your officious exterior you've been hiding a comedienne all this time. For five years you've worked at my side and never let so much as a hint of this whimsical side of your personality out into the open. Whatever could have changed?"

He knows. The little voice inside her was certain— and terrified.

But it was impossible. Valentina knew it was impossible, so she made herself smile and relax against the leather seat as if she'd never in her life been so at her ease. Very much as if she was not within scant inches of a very large, very powerful, very intense male who was eyeing her the way gigantic lions and tigers and jaguars eyed their food. When they were playing with it.

She'd watched enough documentaries and made enough state visits to African countries to know firsthand.

"Perhaps I've always been this amusing," she suggested, managing to tamp down her hysteria about oversize felines, none of which was particularly helpful at the moment. "Perhaps you've only recently allowed yourself to truly listen to me."

"I greatly enjoy listening to you," Achilles replied. There was a laziness in the way he sat there, sprawled out in the backseat of his car, that dark gold gaze on hers. A certain laziness, yes—but Valentina didn't believe it for a second. "I particularly enjoy listening to you when you are doing your job perfectly. Because you know how much I admire perfection. I insist on it, in fact. Which is why I cannot understand why you failed to provide it today."

"I don't know what you mean."

But she knew what he meant. She'd been on the plane and she'd been the one to fail repeatedly to do what was clearly her job. She'd hung up on one conference call and failed entirely to connect another. She'd expected him to explode—if she was honest, there was a part of her that wanted him to explode, in the way that anyone might want to poke and poke and poke at some kind of blister to see if it would pop. But he hadn't popped. He hadn't lost his temper at all, despite the fact that it had been very clear to Valentina very quickly that she was a complete and utter disaster at doing whatever it was that Natalie did.

When Achilles had stared at her in amazement, however, she hadn't made any excuses. She'd only gazed right back, serenely, as if she'd meant to do whatever utterly incorrect thing it was. As if it was all some kind of strategy.

She could admit that she hadn't really thought the job part through. She been so busy fantasizing herself into some kind of normal life that it had never occurred to her that, normal or not, a life was still *a whole life*. She had no idea how to live any way but the way she'd been living for almost thirty years. How remarkably condescending, she'd thought up there on

Achilles Casilieris's jet, that she'd imagined she could simply step into a job—especially one as demanding as this appeared to be—and do it merely because she'd decided it was her chance at something "normal."

Valentina had found the entire experience humbling, if she was honest, and it had been only a few hours since she'd switched places with Natalie in London. Who knew what else awaited her?

But Achilles was still sprawled there beside her, that unnerving look of his making her skin feel too small for her bones.

"Natalie, Natalie," he murmured, and Valentina told herself it was a good thing he'd used that name. It wasn't her name, and she needed the reminder. This wasn't about her. It wasn't her job to advocate for Natalie when the other woman might not wish for her to do anything like that. She was on a fast track to losing Natalie her job, and then what? Valentina didn't have to worry about her employment prospects, but she had no idea what the market was like for billionaire's assistants.

But maybe there was a part of her that already knew that there was no way Natalie Monette was a stranger to her. Certainly not on the genetic level. And that had implications she wasn't prepared to examine just yet, but she did know that the woman who was in all likelihood her long-lost identical twin did not have to work for Achilles Casilieris unless she wanted to.

How arrogant of you, a voice inside her said quietly. *Her Royal Highness, making unilateral decisions for others' lives without their input.*

The voice sounded a little too much like her father's.

"That is my name," Valentina said to Achilles, in case there had been any doubt. Perhaps with a little too much force.

But she had the strangest notion that he was...*tasting* the name as he said it. As if he'd never said it before. Did he call Natalie by her first name? Valentina rather thought not, given that he'd called her *Miss Monette* when she'd met him—but that was neither here nor there, she told herself. And no matter that she was a woman who happened to know the power of titles. She had many of her own. And her life was marked by those who used the different versions of her titles, not to mention the few who actually called her by her first name.

"I cannot tolerate this behavior," he said, but it wasn't in that same infuriated tone he'd used earlier. If anything, he sounded almost...indulgent. But surely that was impossible. "It borders on open rebellion, and I cannot have that. This is not a democracy, I'm afraid. This is a dictatorship. If I want your opinion, I'll tell you what it is."

There was no reason her heart should have been kicking at her like that, her pulse so loud in her ears she was sure he must be able to hear it himself.

"What an interesting way to foster employee loyalty," she murmured. "Really more of a scorch-the-earth approach. Do you find it gets you the results you want?"

"I do not need to breed employee loyalty," Achilles told her, sounding even lazier than before, those dark eyes of his on hers. "People are loyal to me or they are fired. You seem to have forgotten reality today, Natalie. Allow me to remind you that I pay you so much money that I own your loyalty, just as I own everything else."

"Perhaps," and her voice was a little too rough then. A little too shaky, when what could this possibly have to do with her? She was a visitor. Natalie's loyalty was no concern of hers. "I have no wish to be owned. Does anyone? I think you'll find that they do not."

Achilles shrugged. "Whether you wish it or do not, that is how it is."

"That is why I was considering quitting," she heard herself say. And she was no longer looking at him. That was still far too dangerous, too disconcerting. She found herself staring down at her hands, folded in her lap. She could feel that she was frowning, when she learned a long, long time ago never to show her feelings in public. "It's all very well and good for you, of course. I imagine it's quite pleasant to have minions. But for me, there's more to life than blind loyalty. There's more to life than work." She blinked back a strange heat. "I may not have experienced it myself, but I know there must be."

"And what do you think is out there?" He shifted in the seat beside her, but Valentina still refused to look back at him, no matter how she seemed almost physically compelled to do just that. "What do you think you're missing? Is it worth what you are throwing away here today, with this aggressive attitude and the childish pretense that you don't know your own job?"

"It's only those who are bored of the world, or jaded,

who are so certain no one else could possibly wish to see it."

"No one is keeping you from roaming about the planet at will," he told her in a low voice. Too low. So low it danced along her skin and seemed to insinuate itself beneath her flesh. "But you seem to wish to burn down the world you know in order to see the one you don't. That is not what I would call wise. Would you?"

Valentina didn't understand why his words seemed to beat beneath her own skin. But she couldn't seem to catch her breath. And her eyes seemed entirely too full, almost scratchy, with an emotion she couldn't begin to name.

She was aware of too many things. Of the car as it slid through the Manhattan streets. Of Achilles himself, too big and too masculine in the seat beside her, and much too close besides. And most of all, that oddly weighted thing within her, rolling around and around until she couldn't tell the difference between sensation and reaction.

And him right there in the middle of it, confusing her all the more.

CHAPTER THREE

ACHILLES DIDN'T SAY another word, and that was worse. It left Valentina to sit there with her own thoughts in a whirl and nothing to temper them. It left no barrier between that compelling, intent look in his curiously dark eyes and her.

Valentina had no experience with men. Her father had insisted that she grow up as sheltered as possible from public life, so that she could enjoy what little privacy was afforded to a European princess before she turned eighteen. She'd attended carefully selected boarding schools run strictly and deliberately, but that hadn't prevented her classmates from involving themselves in all kinds of dramatic situations. Even then, Valentina had kept herself apart.

Your mother's defection was a stain on the throne, her father always told her. *It is upon us to render it clean and whole again.*

Valentina had been far too terrified of staining Murin any further to risk a scandal. She'd concentrated on her studies and her friends and left the teenage rebellions to others. And once out of school, she'd been thrust unceremoniously into the spotlight. She'd been an ambassador for her kingdom wherever she went, and more than that, she'd always known that she was promised to the Crown Prince of Tissely. Any scandals she embroiled herself in would haunt two kingdoms.

She'd never seen the point.

And along the way she'd started to take a certain pride in the fact that she was saving herself for her predetermined marriage. It was the one thing that was hers to give on her wedding night that had nothing to do with her father or her kingdom.

Is it pride that's kept you chaste—or is it control? a little voice inside her asked then, and the way it kicked in her, Valentina suspected she wouldn't care for the answer. She ignored it.

But the point was, she had no idea how to handle men. Not on any kind of intimate level. These past few hours, in fact, were the longest she'd ever spent alone in the company of a man. It simply didn't happen when she was herself. There were always attendants and aides swarming around Princess Valentina. Always.

She told herself that was why she was having such trouble catching her breath. It was the novelty—that was all. It certainly wasn't *him*.

Still, it was almost a relief when the car pulled up in front of a quietly elegant building on the Upper West Side of Manhattan, perched there with a commanding view of Central Park, and came to a stop.

The late-afternoon breeze washed over her when she stepped from the car, smelling improbably of flowers in the urban sprawl of New York City. But Valentina decided to take it as a blessing.

Achilles remained silent as he escorted her into the building. He only raised his chin in the barest of responses to the greeting that came his way from the doormen in the shiny, obviously upscale lobby, and then he led her into a private elevator located toward the back and behind another set of security guards. It was a gleaming, shining thing that he operated with a key. And it was blessedly without any mirrors.

Valentina wasn't entirely sure whom she'd see if she looked at her own reflection just then.

There were too many things she didn't understand churning inside her, and she hadn't the slightest idea what she was doing here. What on earth she hoped to gain from this odd little lark across the planet, literally in another woman's shoes.

A break, she reminded herself sternly. A vacation. A little holiday away from all the duties and responsibilities of Princess Valentina, which was more important now than ever. She would give herself over to her single-greatest responsibility in a matter of weeks. She would marry Prince Rodolfo and make both of their fathers and all of their subjects very, very happy.

And a brief escape had sounded like bliss for that split second back there in London—and it still did, when she thought about what waited for her. The terribly appropriate royal marriage. The endlessly public yet circumspect life of a modern queen. The glare of all that attention that she and any children she bore could expect no matter where they went or what they did, yet she could never comment upon lest she seem ungrateful or entitled.

Hers was to wave and smile—that was all. She was marrying a man she hardly knew who would expect the marital version of the same. This was a little breather before the reality of all that. This was a tiny bit of space between her circumscribed life at her father's side and more of the same at her husband's.

She couldn't allow the brooding, unreadable man beside her to ruin it, no matter how unnerving his dark gold gaze was. No matter what fires it kicked up inside her that she hardly dared name.

The elevator doors slid open, delivering them straight into the sumptuous front hall of an exquisitely decorated penthouse. Valentina followed Achilles as he strode deep inside, not bothering to spare her a glance as he moved. She was glad that he walked ahead of her, which allowed her to look around so she could get her bearings without seeming to do so. Because, of course, Natalie would already know her way around this place.

She took in the high ceilings and abundant windows all around. The sweeping stairs that led up toward at least two more floors. The mix of art deco and a deep coziness that suggested this penthouse was more than just a showcase; Achilles actually *lived* here.

Valentina told herself—sternly—that there was no earthly reason that notion should make her shiver.

She was absurdly grateful when a housekeeper appeared, clucking at Achilles in what it took Valentina longer than it should have to realize was Greek. A language she could converse in, though she would never consider herself anything like fluent. Still, it took her only a very few moments to understand that whatever the danger Achilles exuded and however ruthless the swath he cut through the entire world with a single glance, this woman thought he was wonderful.

She *beamed* at him.

It would not do to let that get to her, Valentina warned herself as something warm seemed to roll its way through her, pooling in the strangest places. She should not draw any conclusions about a man who was renowned for his fierceness in all things and yet let a housekeeper treat him like family.

The woman declared she would feed him no matter if he was hungry or not, lest he get skinny and weak, and bustled back in the direction of what Valentina assumed was the kitchen.

"You're looking around as if you are lost," Achilles murmured, when Valentina didn't think she'd been looking around at all. "When you have spent more time in this penthouse over the last five years than I have."

Valentina hated the fact that she started a bit when she realized his attention was focused on her again. And that he was speaking in English, which seemed to make him sound that much more knowing.

Or possibly even mocking, unless she was very much mistaken.

"Mr. Casilieris," she said, lacing her voice with gentle reprove, "I work for you. I don't understand why you appear to be quite so interested in what you think is happening inside my head today. Especially when you are so mistaken."

"Am I?"

"Entirely." She raised her brows at him. "If I could suggest that we concentrate more on matters of business than fictional representations of what might or might not be going on inside my mind, I think we might be more productive."

"As productive as we were on the flight over?" His voice was a lazy sort of lash, as amused as it was on target.

Valentina only smiled, hoping she looked enigmatic and strategic rather than at a loss.

"Are *you* lost?" she asked him after a moment, because neither one of them had moved from the great entry that bled into the spacious living room, then soared up two stories, a quiet testament to his wealth and power.

"Careful, Miss Monette," Achilles said with a certain dark precision. "As delightful as I have found today's descent into insubordination, I have a limit. It would be in your best interests not to push me there too quickly."

Valentina had made a study out of humbly accepting all kinds of news she didn't wish to hear over the years. She bent her head, let her lips curve a bit—but not enough to be called a smile, only enough to show she was feeling…something. Then she simply stood there quietly. It was amazing how many unpleasant moments she'd managed to get through that way.

So she had no earthly idea why there was a part of her that wanted nothing more than to look Achilles straight in his dark eyes and ask him, *Or what?*

Somehow, thankfully, she refrained.

Servants came in behind them with luggage—some of which Valentina assumed must be Natalie's and thus hers—but Achilles did not appear to notice them. He kept his attention trained directly on her.

A lesser woman would have been disconcerted, Valentina thought. Someone unused to being the focus of attention, for example. Someone who hadn't spent a part of every day since she turned eighteen having cameras in her face to record every flutter of her eyelashes and rip apart every facet of whatever she happened to be wearing and how she'd done her hair. Every expression that crossed her face was a headline.

What was a cranky billionaire next to that?

"There's no need to repair to our chambers after the flight, I think," he said softly, and Valentina had that odd notion again. That he could see right through her. That he knew things he couldn't possibly know. "We can get right to it."

And there was no reason that that should feel almost…dirty. As if he was suggesting—

But, of course, that was absurd, Valentina told herself staunchly. He was Achilles Casilieris. He was renowned almost as much for his prowess in the sheets as he was for his dominance in the boardroom. In some circles, more.

He tended toward the sort of well-heeled women who were mainstays on various charity circuits. Not for him the actresses or models whom so many other men of his stature preferred. That, apparently, was not good enough for Achilles Casilieris. Valentina had found

herself with some time on the plane to research it herself, after Achilles had finished the final call she'd
failed entirely to set up to his liking and had sat a while,
a fulminating stare fixed on her. Then he'd taken himself off to one of the jet's finely appointed staterooms,
and she'd breathed a bit easier.

A bit.

She'd looked around for a good book to read, pref-
erably a paperback romance because who didn't like
hope and happiness with a bit of sex thrown in to
make it spicy, but there had been nothing of the sort.
Achilles apparently preferred dreary economic magazines that trumpeted out recession and doom from all
quarters. Valentina had kicked off her shoes, tucked
her legs beneath her on the smooth leather chair she'd
claimed for the flight, and indulged herself with a descent into the tabloid and gossip sites she normally
avoided. Because she knew how many lies they told
about her, so why would she believe anything she read
about anyone else?

Still, they were a great way to get a sense of the kind
of coverage a man like Achilles suffered, which would
surely tell her...something. But the answer was...not
much. He was featured in shots from charity events
where other celebrities gathered like cows at a trough,
but was otherwise not really a tabloid staple. Possibly
because he was so sullen and scowling, she thought.

His taste in bedmates, however, was clear even without being splashed across screeching front pages all
over the world. Achilles tended toward women who
were less celebrated for their faces and more for their

actions. Which wasn't to say they weren't all beautiful, of course. That seemed to be a requirement. But they couldn't only be beautiful.

This one was a civil rights attorney of some renown. That one was a journalist who spent most of her time in terrifying war zones. This one had started a charity to benefit a specific cancer that had taken her younger sister. That one was a former Olympic athlete who had dedicated her post-competition life to running a lauded program for at-risk teenagers.

He clearly had a type. Accomplished, beautiful women who did good in the world and who also happened to be wealthy enough all on their own. The uncharitable part of her suspected that last part was because he knew a woman of independent means would not be as interested in his fortune as a woman who had nothing. No gold diggers need apply, clearly.

But the point was, she knew she was mistaken about his potentially suggestive words. Because "assistant to billionaire" was not the kind of profession that would appeal to a man like Achilles. It saved no lives. It bettered nothing.

Valentina found herself glaring at his back as he led her into a lavish office suite on the first level of his expansive penthouse. When she stood in the center of the room, awaiting further instructions, he only crooked a brow. He leaned back against the large desk that stretched across one wall and regarded her with that hot sort of focus that made everything inside her seem to shift hard to the left.

She froze. And then she could have stood there for

hours, for all she knew, as surely as if he'd caught her and held her fast in his fists.

"When you are ready, Miss Monette, feel free to take your seat." His voice was razor sharp, cut through with that same rough darkness that she found crept through her limbs. Lighting her up and making her feel something like sluggish. She didn't understand it. "Though I do love being kept waiting."

More chastened than she wanted to admit, Valentina moved to one of the seats set around a table to the right of the desk, at the foot of towering bookshelves stuffed full of serious-looking books, and settled herself in it. When he continued to stare at her as if she was deliberately keeping him waiting, she reached into the bag—Natalie's bag, which she'd liberated from the bathroom when she'd left the airport with Achilles—until she found a tablet.

A few texts with her double had given her the passwords she needed and some advice.

Just write down everything he says. He likes to forget he said certain things, and it's always good to have a record. One of my jobs is to function as his memory.

Valentina had wanted to text back her thoughts on that, but had refrained. Natalie might have wanted to quit this job, but that was up to her, not the woman taking her place for a few weeks.

"Anything else?" Achilles's voice had a dark edge. "Would you like to have a snack? Perhaps a brief nap? Tell me, is there any way that I can make you more comfortable, Miss Monette, such that you might actually take it upon yourself to do a little work today?"

And Valentina didn't know what came over her. Because she wanted to argue. She, who had made a virtue out of remaining quiet and cordial under any circumstances, wanted to fight. She didn't understand it. She knew it was Achilles. That there was something in him that made her want to do or say anything to get some kind of reaction. It didn't matter that it was madness. It was something about that look in his eyes. Something about that hard, amused mouth of his.

It was something about *him*.

But Valentina reminded herself that this was not her life.

This was not her life and this was not her job, and none of this was hers to ruin. She was the steward of Natalie's life for a little while, nothing more. She imagined that Natalie would be doing the same for her. Maybe breathing a little bit of new life into the tired old royal nonsense she'd find waiting for her at Murin Castle, but that was all. Neither one of them was out to wreck what they found.

And she'd never had any trouble whatsoever keeping to the party line. Doing her father's bidding, behaving appropriately, being exactly the princess whom everyone imagined she was. She felt that responsibility—to her people, to her bloodline, to her family's history— deeply. She'd never acted out the way so many of her friends had. She'd never fought against her own responsibilities. It wasn't that she was afraid to do any of those things, but simply that it had never occurred to her to try. Valentina had always known exactly who she was and what her life would hold, from her earliest days.

So she didn't recognize this thing in her that wanted nothing more than to cause a commotion. To stand up and throw the tablet she held at Achilles's remarkably attractive head. To kick over the chair she was sitting in and, while she was at it, that desk of his, too, all brash steel and uncompromising masculinity, just like its owner.

She wanted to do *something*. Anything. She could feel it humming through her veins, bubbling in her blood. As if something about this normal life she'd tried on for size had infected her. Changed her. When it had only been a few hours.

He's a ruthless man, something reckless inside her whispered. *He can take it.*

But this wasn't her life. She had to protect it, not destroy it, no matter what was moving in her, poking at her, tempting her to act out for the first time in her life.

So Valentina smiled up at Achilles, forced herself to remain serene the way she always did, and got to work.

It was late into the New York night when Achilles finally stopped torturing his deceitful princess.

He made her go over byzantine contracts that rendered his attorneys babbling idiots. He questioned her on clauses he only vaguely understood himself, and certainly couldn't expect her to be conversant on. He demanded she prepare memos he had no intention of sending. He questioned her about events he knew she could not possibly know anything about, and the truth was that he enjoyed himself more than he could remember enjoying anything else for quite some time.

When Demetria had bustled in with food, Achilles had waved Valentina's away.

"My assistant does not like to eat while she works," he told his housekeeper, but he'd kept his gaze on Valentina while he'd said it.

"I don't," she'd agreed merrily enough. "I consider it a weakness." She'd smiled at him. "But you go right ahead."

Point to the princess, he'd thought.

The most amazing thing was that Princess Valentina never backed down. Her ability to brazen her way through the things she didn't know, in fact, was nothing short of astounding. Impressive in the extreme. Achilles might have admired it if he hadn't been the one she was trying to fool.

"It is late," he said finally, when he thought her eyes might glaze over at last. Though he would cast himself out his own window to the Manhattan streets below before he'd admit his might, too. "And while there is always more to do, I think it is perhaps wise if we take this as a natural stopping place."

Valentina smiled at him, tucked up in that chair of hers that she had long since claimed as her own in a way he couldn't remember the real Natalie had ever done, her green eyes sparkling.

"I understand if you need a rest," she said sweetly. Too sweetly. "Sir."

Achilles had been standing at the windows, his back to the mad gleam of Manhattan. But at that, he let

himself lean back, his body shifting into something…
looser. More dangerous.

And much, much hotter than contracts.

"I worry my hearing has failed me. Because it
sounded very much as if you were impugning my
manhood."

"Only if your manhood is so fragile that you can't
imagine it requires a rest," she said, and aimed a sunny
smile at him as if that would take away the sting of
her words. "But you are Achilles Casilieris. You have
made yourself a monument to manhood, clearly. No
fragility allowed."

"It is almost as if you think debating me like this
is some kind of strategy," he said softly, making no
attempt to ratchet back the ruthlessness in his voice.
Much less do something about the fire he could feel
storming through him everywhere else. "Let me warn
you, again, it is only a strategy if your goal is to find
yourself without a job and without a recommendation.
To say nothing of the black mark I will happily put beside your name."

Valentina waved a hand in the air, airily, dismiss-
ing him. And her possible firing, black marks—all of
it. Something else he very likely would have found
impressive if he'd been watching her do it to someone else.

"So many threats." She shook her head. "I understand that this is how you run your business and you're
very successful, but really. It's exhausting. Imagine
how many more bees you could get with honey."

He didn't want to think about honey. Not when there

were only the two of them here, in this office cushioned by the night outside and the rest of the penthouse. No shared walls on these floors he owned. This late, none of the staff would be up. It was only Achilles and this princess pretending to be his assistant, and the buttery light of the few lamps they'd switched on, making the night feel thick and textured everywhere the light failed to reach.

Like inside him.

"Come here."

Valentina blinked, but her green gaze was unreadable then. She only looked at him for a moment, as if she'd forgotten that she was playing this game. And that in it, she was his subordinate.

"Come here," he said again. "Do not make me repeat myself, I beg you. You will not like my response."

She stood the way she did everything else, with an easy grace. With that offhanded elegance that did things to him he preferred not to examine. And he knew she had no desire to come any closer to him. He could feel it. Her wariness hung between them like some kind of smoke, and it ignited that need inside him. And for a moment he thought she might disobey him. That she might balk—and it was in that moment he thought she'd stay where she was, across the room, that he had understood how very much he wanted her.

In a thousand ways he shouldn't, because Achilles was a man who did not *want*. He took. Wanting was a weakness that led only to darkness—though it didn't feel like a weakness tonight. It felt like the opposite.

But he'd underestimated his princess. Her shoulders straightened almost imperceptibly. And then she glided toward him, head high like some kind of prima ballerina, her face set in the sort of pleasant expression he now knew she could summon and dispatch at will. He admired that, too.

And he'd thrown out that summons because he could. Because he wanted to. And he was experimenting with this new *wanting*, no matter how little he liked it.

Still, there was no denying the way his body responded as he watched her walk toward him. There was no denying the rich, layered tension that seemed to fill the room. And him, making his pulse a living thing as his blood seemed to heat in his veins.

Something gleamed in that green gaze of hers, but she kept coming. She didn't stop until she was directly beside him, so close that if she breathed too heavily he thought her shoulder might brush his. He shifted so that he stood slightly behind her, and jutted his chin toward the city laid out before them.

"What do you see when you look out the window?"

He felt more than saw the glance she darted at him. But then she kept her eyes on the window before them. On the ropes of light stretching out in all hectic directions possible below.

"Is that a trick question? I see Manhattan."

"I grew up in squalor." His voice was harsher than he'd intended, but Achilles did nothing to temper it. "It is common, I realize, for successful men to tell stories of their humble beginnings. Americans in particular find these stories inspiring. It allows them to fantasize that they, too, might better themselves against any odds. But the truth is more of a gray area, is it not? Beginnings are never quite so humble as they sound when rich men claim them. But me?" He felt her gaze on him then, instead of the mess of lights outside. "When I use the word *squalor*, that's an upgrade."

Her swallow was audible. Or perhaps he was paying her too close attention. Either way, he didn't back away.

"I don't know why you're telling me this."

"When you look through this window you see a city. A place filled with people going about their lives, traffic and isolation." He shifted so he could look down at her. "I see hope. I see vindication. I see all the despair and all the pain and all the loss that went into creating the man you see before you tonight. Creating this." And he moved his chin to indicate the penthouse. And the Casilieris Company while he was at it. "And there is nothing that I wouldn't do to protect it."

And he didn't know what had happened to him while he was speaking. He'd been playing a game, and then suddenly it seemed as if the game had started to play him—and it wasn't finished. Something clutched at him, as if he was caught in the grip of some massive fist.

It was almost as if he wanted this princess, this woman who believed she was tricking him—deceiving him—to understand him.

This, too, was unbearable.

But he couldn't seem to stop.

"Do you think people become driven by accident, Miss Monette?" he asked, and he couldn't have said why that thing gripping him seemed to clench harder. Making him sound far more intense than he thought he should have felt. Risking the truth about himself he carried inside and shared with no one. But he still didn't stop. "Ambition, desire, focus and drive—do you think these things grow on trees? But then, perhaps I'm asking the wrong person. Have you not told me a thousand times that you are not personally ambitious?"

It was one of the reasons he'd kept Natalie with him for so long, when other assistants to men like him used positions like hers as springboards into their own glorious careers. But this woman was not Natalie. If he hadn't known it before, he'd have known it now, when it was a full-scale struggle to keep his damned hands to himself.

"Ambition, it seems to me, is for those who have the freedom to pursue it. And for those who do not—" and Valentina's eyes seemed to gleam at that, making Achilles wonder exactly what her ambitions were "—it is nothing more than dissatisfaction. Which is far less worthy and infinitely more destructive, I think we can agree."

He didn't know when he'd turned to face her fully. He didn't know when he'd stopped looking at the city and was looking only at her instead. But he was, and he compounded that error by reaching out his hand and tugging on the very end of her silky, coppery ponytail where it kissed her shoulder every time she moved her head.

Her lips parted, as if on a soundless breath, and Achilles felt that as if she'd caressed him. As if her hands were on his body the way he wished they were, instead of at her sides.

"Are you dissatisfied?" It was amazing how difficult it was not to use her real name then. How challenging it was to stay in this game he suddenly didn't particularly want to play. "Is that what this is?"

Her green eyes, which had been so unreadable, suddenly looked slick. Dark and glassy with some or other emotion. He couldn't tell what it was, and still, he could feel it in him like smoke, stealing through his chest and making it harder than it should have been to breathe.

"There's nothing wrong with dissatisfaction in and of itself," she told him after a moment, then another, that seemed too large for him to contain. Too dark and much too edgy to survive intact, and yet here they both were. "You see it as disloyalty, but it's not."

"How can it be anything else?"

"It is possible to be both loyal and open to the possibility that there is a life outside the one you've committed yourself to." Her green eyes searched his. "Surely there must be."

"I think you will find that there is no such possibility." His voice was harsh. He could feel it inside him, like a stain. Like need. "We must all decide who we are, every moment of every day. You either keep a vow or you do not. There is no between."

She stiffened at that, then tried to force her shoulders back down to an easier, less telling angle. Achilles watched her do it. He watched something like distress cross her lovely face, but she hid that, too. It was only the darkness in her gaze that told him he'd scored a direct hit, and he was a man who took great pride in the strikes he leveled against anyone who tried to move against him. Yet what he felt when he looked at Valentina was not pride. Not pride at all.

"Some vows are not your own," she said fiercely, her gaze locked to his. "Some are inherited. It's easy to say that you'll keep them because that's what's expected of you, but it's a great deal harder to actually *do* it."

He knew the vows she'd made. That pointless prince. Her upcoming royal wedding. He assumed that was the least of the vows she'd inherited from her father. And he still thought it was so much smoke and mirrors to hide the fact that she, like so many of her peers, was a spoiled and pampered creature who didn't like to be told what to do. Wasn't that the reason *poor little rich girl* was a saying in the first place?

He had no sympathy for the travails of a rich, pampered princess. But he couldn't seem to unwind that little silken bit of copper from around his finger, either. Much less step back and put the space between them that he should have left there from the start.

Achilles shook his head. "There is no gray area. Surely you know this. You are either who you say you are or you are not."

There was something like misery in those eyes of hers then. And this was what he'd wanted. This was why he'd been goading her. And yet now that he seemed to have succeeded, he felt the strangest thing deep in his gut. It was an unpleasant and unfamiliar sensation, and at first Achilles couldn't identify it. It was a low heat, trickling through him, making him restless. Making him as close to uncertain as he'd ever been.

In someone else, he imagined, it might be shame. But shame was not something Achilles allowed in himself. Ever.

This was a night full of things he did not allow, apparently. Because he wanted her. He wanted to punctuate this oddly emotional discussion with his mouth. His hands. The whole of his too-tight, too-interested body pressed deep into hers. He wanted to taste those sweetly lush lips of hers. He wanted to take her elegant face in his hands, tip her head back and sate himself at last. It seemed to him an age or two since he'd boarded his plane and realized his assistant was not who she was supposed to be. An agony of waiting and all that *want*, and he was not a man who agonized. Or waited. Or wanted anything, it seemed, but this princess who thought she could fool him.

What was the matter with him that some part of him wanted to let her?

He did none of the things he longed to do.

Achilles made himself do the hard thing, no matter how complicated it was. Or how complicated it felt, anyway. When really it was so simple. He let her go. He let her silky hair fall from between his fingers, and he stepped back, putting inches between them.

But that did nothing to ease the temptation.

"I think what you need is a good night's sleep," he told her, like some kind of absurd nurturer. Something he had certainly never tried to be for anyone else in the whole of his life. He would have doubted it was possible—and he refused to analyze that. "Perhaps it will clear your head and remind you of who you are. Jet lag can make that so very confusing, I know."

He thought she might have scuttled from the room at that, filled with her own shame if there was any decency in the world, but he was learning that this princess was not at all who he expected her to be. She swallowed, hard. And he could still see that darkness in her eyes. But she didn't look away from him. And she certainly didn't scuttle anywhere.

"I know exactly who I am, Mr. Casilieris," she said, very directly, and the lenses in her glasses made her eyes seem that much greener. "As I'm certain you do, too. Jet lag makes a person tired. It doesn't make them someone else entirely."

And when she turned to walk from the room then, it was with her head held high, graceful and self-contained, with no apparent second thoughts. Or anything the least bit like shame. All he could read on her as she went was that same distracting elegance that was already too far under his skin.

Achilles couldn't seem to do a thing but watch her go.

And when the sound of her footsteps had faded away, deep into the far reaches of the penthouse, he turned back to the wild gleam of Manhattan on the other side of his windows. Frenetic and frenzied. Light in all directions, as if there was nothing more to the world tonight than this utterly mad tangle of life and traffic and people and energy and it hardly mattered what he felt so high above it. It hardly mattered at all that he'd betrayed himself. That this woman who should have been nothing to him made him act like someone he barely recognized.

And her words stayed with him. *I know exactly who I am.* They echoed around and around in his head until it sounded a whole lot more like an accusation.

As if she was the one playing this game, and winning it, after all.

CHAPTER FOUR

As the days passed, Valentina thought that she was getting the hang of this assistant thing—especially if she endeavored to keep a minimum distance between herself and Achilles when the night got a little too dark and close. And at all other times, for that matter.

She'd chalked up those odd, breathless moments in his office that first night to the strangeness of inhabiting someone else's life. Because it couldn't be anything else. Since then, she hadn't felt the need to say too much. She hadn't defended herself—or her version of Natalie. She'd simply tried to do the job that Natalie, apparently, did so well she was seen by other employees of the Casilieris Company as superhuman.

With every day she became more accustomed to the demands of the job. She felt less as if she really ought to have taken Achilles up on his offer of a parachute and more as if this was something she could handle. Maybe not well or like superhuman Natalie, but she could handle it all the same in her own somewhat rudimentary fashion.

What she didn't understand was why Achilles hadn't

fired her already. Because it was perfectly clear to Valentina that her version of handling things in no way lived up to Achilles's standards.

And if she'd been any doubt about that, he was the first to tell her otherwise.

His corporate offices in Manhattan took up several floors at one of Midtown's most esteemed addresses. There was an office suite set aside for him, naturally enough, that sprawled across the top floor and looked out over Manhattan as if to underscore the notion that Achilles Casilieris was in every way on top of the world. Valentina was settled in the immediate outer office, guarded by two separate lines of receptionist and secretarial defense should anyone make it through security. It wasn't to protect Achilles, but to further illuminate his importance. And Natalie's, Valentina realized quickly.

Because Natalie controlled access to Achilles. She controlled his schedule. She answered his phone and his email, and was generally held to have that all-important insight into his moods.

"What kind of day is it?" the senior vice presidents would ask her as they came in for their meetings, and the fact they smiled as they said it didn't make them any less anxious to hear her answer.

Valentina quickly discovered that Natalie controlled a whole lot more than simple access. There was a steady line of people at her desk, coming to her to ask how best to approach Achilles with any number of issues, or plot how to avoid approaching him with the things they knew he'd hate. Over the course of her first week in New York City, Valentina found that almost everyone who worked for Achilles tried to run things past her first, or used her to gauge his reactions. Natalie was less the man's personal assistant, she realized, and more the hub around which his businesses revolved. More than that, she thought he knew it.

"Take that up with Natalie," he would say in the middle of a meeting, without even bothering to look over at her. Usually while cutting someone off, because even he appeared not to want to hear certain things until Natalie had assessed them first.

"Come up with those numbers and run them past Natalie," he would tell his managers, and sometimes he'd even sound irritated while he said such things.

"Why are you acting as if you have never worked a day in my company?" he'd demanded of one of his brand managers once. "I am not the audience for your uncertain first drafts, George. How can you not know this?"

Valentina had smiled at the man in the meeting, and then had been forced to sit through a brainstorming/therapy session with him afterward, all the while hoping that the noncommittal things she'd murmured were, at the very least, not the *opposite* of the sort of things Natalie might have said.

Not that she texted Natalie to find out. Because that might have led to a conversation Valentina didn't really want to have with her double about strange, tense moments in the darkness with her employer.

She didn't know what she was more afraid of. That Natalie had never had any kind of tension with Achilles and Valentina was messing up her entire life…or that she did. That *tension* was just what Achilles did.

Valentina concentrated on her first attempt at a normal life, complete with a normal job, instead. And whether Achilles was aware of it or not, Natalie had her fingers in everything.

Including his romantic life.

The first time Valentina had answered his phone to find an emotional woman on the other end, she'd been appalled.

"There's a crying woman on the phone," she'd told Achilles. It had taken her a day or so to realize that she wasn't only allowed to walk in and out of his office when necessary, but encouraged to do so. That particular afternoon Achilles had been sitting on the sofa in his office, his feet up on his coffee table as he'd scowled down at his laptop. He shifted that scowl to her instead, in a way that made Valentina imagine that whatever he was looking at had something to do with her—

But that was ridiculous. There was no *her* in this scenario. There was only Natalie, and Valentina very much doubted Achilles spent his time looking up his assistant on the internet.

"Why are you telling me this?" he'd asked her shortly. "If I wanted to know who called me, I would answer my phones myself."

"She's crying about you," Valentina had said. "I assume she's calling to share her emotions with you, the person who caused them."

"And I repeat—why are you telling me this." This time it wasn't a question, and his scowl deepened. "You are my assistant. You are responsible for fielding these calls. I'm shocked you're even mentioning another crying female. I thought you stopped bringing them to my attention years ago."

Valentina had blinked at that. "Aren't you at all interested in why this woman is upset?"

"No."

"Not at all. Not the slightest bit interested." She studied his fierce face as if he was an alien. In moments like this, she thought he must have been. "You don't even know which woman I'm referring to, do you?"

"Miss Monette." He bit out that name as if the taste of it irritated him, and Valentina couldn't have said why it put her back up when it wasn't even her name. "I have a number of mistresses, none of whom call that line to manufacture emotional upsets. You are already aware of this." And he'd set his laptop aside, as if he needed to concentrate fully on Valentina before him. It had made her spine prickle, from her neck to her bottom and back up again. "Please let me know exactly what agenda it is we are pursuing today, that you expect to interrupt me in order to have a discussion about nuisance calls. When I assure you, the subject does not interest me at all. Just as it did not interest me five years ago, when you vowed to stop bothering me about them."

There was a warning in that. Valentina had heard it, plain as day. But she hadn't been able to heed it. Much less stop herself.

"To be clear, what you're telling me is that tears do not interest you," she'd said instead of beating a retreat to her desk the way she should have. She'd kept her tone even and easy, but she doubted that had fooled either one of them.

"Tears interest me least of all." She'd been sure that there was a curve in that hard mouth of his then, however small.

And what was the matter with her that she'd clung to that as if it was some kind of lifeline? As if she needed such a thing?

As if what she really wanted was his approval, when she hadn't switched places with Natalie for him. He'd had nothing to do with it. Why couldn't she seem to remember that?

"If this is a common occurrence for you, perhaps you need to have a think about your behavior," she'd pointed out. "And your aversion to tears."

There had definitely been a curve in his mouth then, and yet somehow that hadn't made Valentina any easier.

"This conversation is over," he'd said quietly. Though not gently. "Something I suggest you tell the enterprising actress on the phone."

She'd thought him hideously cold, of course. Heartless, even. But the calls kept coming. And Valentina had quickly realized what she should perhaps have known from the start—that it would be impossible for Achilles to actually be out there causing harm to so many anonymous women when he never left the office. She knew this because she spent almost every hour of every day in his company. The man literally had no time to go out there smashing hearts left and right, the way she'd be tempted to believe he did if she paid attention only to the phone calls she received, laden with accusations.

"Tell him I'm falling apart," yet another woman on the phone said on this latest morning, her voice ragged.

"Sorry, but what's your name again?" Valentina asked, as brightly as possible. "It's only that he's been working rather hard, you see. As he tends to do. Which would, of course, make it extremely difficult for him to be tearing anyone apart in any real sense."

The woman had sputtered. But Valentina had dutifully taken her name into Achilles when he next asked for his messages.

"I somewhat doubted the veracity of her claim," Valentina murmured. "Given that you were working until well after two last night."

Something she knew very well since that had meant she'd been working even longer than that.

Achilles laughed. He was at his desk today, which meant he was framed by the vertical thrust of Manhattan behind him. And still, that look in his dark gold gaze made the city disappear. "As well you should. I have no idea who this woman is. Or any of them." He shrugged. "My attorneys are knee-deep in paternity suits, and I win every one of them."

Valentino was astonished by that. Perhaps that was naive. She'd certainly had her share of admirers in her day, strange men who claimed an acquaintance or who sent rather disturbing letters to the palace—some from distant prisons in foreign countries. But she certainly never had men call up and try to pretend they had relationships with her *to* her.

Then again, would anyone have told her if they had? That sat on her a bit uneasily, though she couldn't have said why. She only knew that his gaze was like a touch, and that, too, seemed to settle on her like a weight.

"It's amazlng how many unhinged women seem to think that if they claim they're dating you, you might go along with it," she said before she could think better of it.

That dark gold gaze of his lit with a gleam she couldn't name then. And it sparked something deep inside her, making her fight to draw in a breath. Making her feel unsteady in the serviceable low heels that Natalie favored. Making her wish she'd worn something more substantial than a nice jacket over another pencil skirt. Like a suit of armor. Or her very own brick wall.

"There are always unhinged women hanging about," Achilles said in that quietly devastating way of his. "Trying to convince me that they have relationships with me that they adamantly do not. Why do you imagine that is, Miss Monette?"

She told herself he couldn't possibly know that she was one of those women, no matter how his gaze seemed to pin her where she stood. No matter the edge in his voice, or the sharp emphasis he'd put on *Miss Monette*.

Even if he suspected something was different with his assistant, he couldn't know. Because no one could know. Because Valentina herself hadn't known Natalie existed until she'd walked into that bathroom. And that meant all sorts of things, such as the fact that everything she'd been told about her childhood and her birth was a lie. Not to mention her mother.

But there was no way Achilles could know any of that.

"Perhaps it's you," she murmured in response. She smiled when his brows rose in that expression of sheer arrogance that never failed to make her feel the slightest bit dizzy. "I only mean that you're a public figure and people imagine you a certain way based on the kind of press coverage you allow. Unless you plan to actively get out there and reclaim your public narrative, I don't think there's any likelihood that it will change."

"I am not a public figure. I have never courted the public in any way."

Valentina checked a sigh. "You're a very wealthy man. Whether you like it or not, the public is fascinated by you."

Achilles studied her until she was forced to order herself not to fidget beneath the weight of that heavy, intense stare.

"I'm intrigued that you think the very existence of public fascination must create an obligation in me to cater to it," he said quietly. "It does not. In fact, it has the opposite effect. In me. But how interesting that you imagine you owe something to the faceless masses who admire you."

Valentina's lips felt numb. "No masses, faceless or otherwise, admire me, Mr. Casilieris. They have no idea I exist. I'm an assistant, nothing more."

His hard mouth didn't shift into one of those hard

curves, but his dark gold eyes gleamed, and somehow that made the floor beneath her seem to tilt, then roll.

"Of course you are," he said, his voice a quiet menace that echoed in her like a warning. Like something far more dangerous than a simple warning. "My mistake."

Later that night, still feeling as off balance as if the floor really wasn't steady beneath her feet, Valentina found herself alone with Achilles long after everyone else in the office had gone home.

It had been an extraordinarily long couple of days, something Valentina might have thought was business as usual for the Casilieris Company if so many of the other employees hadn't muttered about how grueling it was. Beneath their breath and when they thought she couldn't hear them, that was. The deal that Achilles was so determined to push through had turned out to have more tangles and turns than anyone had expected—especially, it seemed, Achilles. What that meant was long hour after long hour well into the tiny hours of the night, hunched over tables and conference rooms, arguing with fleets of attorneys and representatives from the other side over take-out food from fine New York restaurants and stale coffee.

Valentina was deep into one of the contracts Achilles had slid her way, demanding a fresh set of eyes on a clause that annoyed him, when she noticed that they were the only ones there. The Casilieris Company had a significant presence all over the planet, so there were usually people coming and going at all conceivable hours to be available to different workdays in distant places. Something Valentina had witnessed herself after spending so much time in these offices since she'd arrived in New York.

But when she looked up from the dense and confusing contract language for a moment to give her ever-impending headache a break, she could see from the long conference room table where she sat straight through the glass walls that allowed her to see all the way across the office floor. And there was no one there. No bustling secretaries, no ambitious VPs putting in ostentatiously late hours where the boss could see their vigilance and commitment. No overzealous interns making busy work for themselves in the cubicles. No late-night cleaning crews, who did their jobs in the dark so as not to bother the workers by day. There wasn't a soul. Anywhere.

Something caught in her chest as she realized that it was only the two of them. Just Valentina and the man across the table from her, whom she was trying very hard not to look at too closely.

It was an extraordinarily unimportant thing to notice, she chastised herself, frowning back down at the contract. They were always alone, really. In his car, on his plane, in his penthouse. Valentina had spent more time with this man, she thought, than with any other save her father.

Her gaze rose from the contract of its own accord. Achilles sat across from her in the quiet of the otherwise empty office, his laptop cracked open before him and a pile of contracts next to the sleek machine. He looked the way he always did at the end of these long days. *Entirely too good*, something in her whispered—though she shoved that aside as best she could. It did no good to concentrate on things like that, she'd decided during her tenure with him. The man's appearance was a fact, and it was something she needed to come to terms with, but she certainly didn't have to ogle him.

But she couldn't seem to look away. She remembered that moment in his penthouse a little too clearly, the first night they'd been in New York. She remembered how close they'd stood in that window, and the things he'd told her, that dark gold gaze of his boring into her. As if he had every intention of looking directly to her soul. More than that, she remembered him reaching out and taking hold of the end of the ponytail she'd worn, that he'd looked at as if he had no idea how it had come to be attached to her.

But she'd dreamed about it almost every time she'd slept, either way.

Tonight Achilles was lounging in a pushed-back chair, his hands on top of his head as if, had he had longer hair, he'd be raking his hands through it. His jaw was dotted with stubble after a long day in the office, and it lent him the look of some kind of pirate.

Valentina told herself—sternly—that there was no need for such fanciful language when he already made her pulse heat inside her simply by being in the same room. She tried to sink down a bit farther behind the piles and piles of documents surrounding her, which she was viewing as the armor she wished she was wearing. The remains of the dinner she'd ordered them many hours before were scattered across the center of the table, and she took perhaps too much pride in the fact she'd completed so simple a task. Normal people, she was certain, ordered from take-out menus all the time, but Valentina never had before she'd taken over Natalie's life. Valentina was a princess. She'd discussed many a menu and sent requests to any number of kitchens, but she'd never ordered her own meal in her life, much less from stereotypical New Yorkers with accents and attitudes.

She felt as if she was in a movie.

Valentina decided she would take her victories where she found them. Even if they were as small and ultimately pointless as sending out for a takeaway meal.

"It's late," Achilles said, reminding her that they were all alone here. And there was something in his voice then. Or the way his gaze slammed into hers when she looked up again.

Or maybe it was in her—that catch. That little kick of something a little too much like excitement that wound around and around inside her. Making her feel…restless. Undone. Desperate for something she couldn't even name.

"And here I thought you planned to carry straight through until dawn," she said, as brightly as possible, hoping against hope he couldn't see anything on her face. Or hear it in her voice.

Achilles lowered his hand to the arms of his chair. But he didn't shift that gaze of his from hers. And she kept catching him looking at her like this. Exactly like this. Simmering. Dark and dangerous, and spun through with gold. In the cars they took together. Every morning when he walked out of his bedchamber and found her sitting in the office suite, already starting on the day's work as best she could. Across boardroom tables just like this one, no matter if they were filled with other people.

It was worse now. Here in the quiet of his empty office. So late at night it felt to Valentina as if the darkness was a part of her.

And Valentina didn't have any experience with men, but oh, the books she'd read. Love stories and romances and happy-ever-afters, and almost all of them started just like this. With a taut feeling in the belly and fire everywhere else.

Do not be absurd, she snapped at herself.

Because she was Princess Valentina of Murin. She was promised to another and had been since her birth. There wasn't space in her life for anything but that. Not even here, in this faraway place that had nothing at all to do with her real life. Not even with this man, whom she never should have met, and never would have had she not seized that moment in the London bathroom.

You can take a holiday from your life, apparently, she reminded herself. *But you still take you along with you wherever you go.*

She might have been playing Natalie Monette, but she was still *herself*. She was still the same person she'd always been. Dutiful. Mindful of what her seemingly inconsequential behavior might mean to her father, to the kingdom, to her future husband's kingdom, too. Whatever else she was—and she wasn't sure she knew anymore, not here in the presence of a man who made her head spin without seeming to try very hard—Valentina was a person who had always, always kept her vows.

Even when it was her father who had made them, not her.

"If you keep staring at me like that," Achilles said softly, a kind of ferociousness beneath his rough words that made her stomach knot, then seemed to kindle a different, deeper fire lower down, "I am not certain I'll be able to contain myself."

Valentina's mouth was dry. "I don't know what you mean."

"I think you do."

Achilles didn't move, she could see that he wasn't moving, and yet everything changed at that. He filled every room he entered—she was used to that by now—but this was something different. It was as if lightning flashed. It was if he was some kind of rolling thunder all his own. It was as if he'd called in a storm, then let it loose to fill all of the room. The office.

And Valentina, too.

"No," she whispered, her voice scratchy against all that light and rumble.

But she could feel the tumult inside her. It was fire and it was light and it threatened to burst free of the paltry cage of her skin. Surely she would burst. Surely no person could survive this. She felt it shake all through her, as if underlining her fear.

"I don't know what you mean, and I don't like what you're implying. I think perhaps we've been in this office too long. You seem to have mistaken me for one of your mistresses. Or worse, one of those desperate women who call in, hoping to convince you they ought to be one of them."

"On the contrary, Miss Monette."

And there was a starkness to Achilles's expression then. No curve on his stern mouth. No gleaming thing in the seductive gold of his dark eyes. But somehow, that only made it worse.

"You're the one who manages my mistresses. And those who pretend to that title. How could I possibly confuse you for them?" He cocked his head slightly to one side, and something yawned open inside her, as if in response. "Or perhaps you're auditioning for the role?"

"No." Her voice was no less scratchy this time, but there was more power in it. *Or more fear*, something inside her whispered. "I am most certainly not auditioning for anything like that. Or anything at all. I already have a job."

"But you told me you meant to quit." She had the strangest notion then that he was enjoying himself. "Perhaps you meant you were looking to make a lateral move. From my boardroom to my bed?"

Valentina tried to summon her outrage. She tried to tell herself that she was deeply offended on Natalie's behalf, because of course this was about her, not Valentina herself... She tried to tell herself a whole lot of things.

But she couldn't quite get there. Instead, she was awash with unhelpful little visions, red hot and wild.

Images of what a "lateral move" might look like. Of what his bed might feel like. Of him.

She imagined that lean, solidly muscled form stretched over hers, the way she'd read in so many books so many times. Something almost too hot to bear melted through her then, pulling deep in her belly, and making her breath go shallow before it shivered everywhere else.

As if it was already happening.

"I know that this might come as a tremendous shock," Valentina said, trying to make herself sound something like fierce—or unmoved, anyway. Anything other than thrown and yearning. "But I have no interest in your bed. Less than no interest."

"You are correct." And something gleamed bright and hot and unholy gold in that dark gaze of his. "I am in shock."

"The next time an aspiring mistress calls the office," Valentina continued coolly, and no matter that it cost her, "I'll be certain to put her through to you for a change. You can discuss lateral moves all day long."

"What if a random caller does not appeal to me?" he asked lazily, as if this was all a game to him. She told herself it was. She told herself the fact that it was a game made it safe, but she didn't believe it. Not when all the things that moved around inside her made it hard to breathe, and made her feel anything at all but *safe*. "What if it is I who wish to alter our working relationship after all these years?"

Valentina told herself that this was clearly a test. If, as this conversation seemed to suggest, Natalie's relationship with her boss had always been strictly professional, why would he want to change that now? She'd seen how distant he kept his romantic entanglements from his work. His work was his life. His women were afterthoughts. There was no way the driven, focused man she'd come to know a bit after the close proximity of these last days would want to muddy the water in his office, with the assistant who not only knew where all the bodies were buried, but oversaw the funeral rites herself.

This had to be a test.

"I don't wish to alter a thing," she told him, very distinctly, as if there was nothing in her head but thorny contract language. And certainly nothing involving that remarkably ridged torso of his. "If you do, I think we should revisit the compensation package on offer for my resignation."

Achilles smiled as if she delighted him. But in an entirely too wicked and too hot sort of way.

"There is no package, Miss Monette," he murmured. "And there will be no resignation. When will you understand? You are here to do as I wish. Nothing more and nothing less than that. And perhaps my wishes concerning your role here have changed."

He wants you to fall apart, Valentina snapped at herself. *He wants to see if this will break you. He's poking at* Natalie *about her change in performance, not at you. He doesn't know* you *exist.*

Because there could be no other explanation. And it didn't matter that the look in his eyes made her shudder, down deep inside.

"Your wishes concerning my role now involve me on my back?" It cost her to keep her voice that flat. She could feel it.

"You say that as if the very idea disgusts you." And that crook in the corner of his lethal mouth deepened, even as that look in his eyes went lethal. "Surely not."

Valentina forced herself to smile. Blandly. As if her heart wasn't trying to claw its way out of her chest.

"I'm very flattered by your offer, of course," she said.

A little too sweetly to be mistaken for sincerity.

Achilles laughed then. It was an unsettling sound, too rough and too bold. It told her too much. That he knew—everything. That he knew all the things that were moving inside her, white hot and molten and too much for her to handle or tamp down or control. There was a growing, impossible fire raging in places she hardly understood, rendering her a stranger to herself.

As if he was the one in control of her body, even sitting across the table, lounging in his seat as if none of this was a matter of any concern at all.

While she felt as if she was both losing pieces of herself—and seeing her true colors for the very first time.

"Are you letting me down easy?" Achilles asked.

There was still laughter in his voice, his gaze and, somehow, dancing in the air between them despite all that fire still licking at her. She felt it roll through her, as if those big hands of his were on her skin.

And then she was suddenly incapable of thinking about anything at all but that. His hands all over her body. Touching places only she had ever seen. She had to swallow hard. Then again. And still there was that ringing in her ears.

"Do think it will work?" he asked, laughter still making his words sound a little too much like the rough, male version of honey.

"I imagine it will work beautifully, yes." She held on to that smile of hers as if her life depended on it. She rather thought it did. It was that or tip over into all that fire, and she had no idea what would become of her if she let that happen. She had no idea what would be left. "Or, of course, I could involve Human Resources in this discussion."

Achilles laughed again, and this time it was rougher. Darker and somehow hotter at the same time. Valentina felt it slide all over her, making her breasts feel heavy and her hips restless. While deep between her legs, a slick ache bloomed.

"I admire the feigned naïveté," Achilles said, and he looked like a pirate again, all dark jaw and that gleam in his gaze. It lit her up. Everywhere. "I have obviously failed to appreciate your acting talent sufficiently. I think we both know what Human Resources will tell you. To suck it up or find another position."

"That does not sound at all like something Human Resources would say," Valentina replied crisply, rather than spending even a split second thinking about *sucking*. "It sounds as if you're laboring under the delusion that this is a cult of personality, not a business."

If she expected him to look at all abashed, his grin disabused her of it. "Do you doubt it?"

"I'm not sure that is something I would brag about, Mr. Casilieris."

His gaze was hot, and she didn't think he was talking about her job or his company any longer. Had he ever been?

"Is it bragging if it's true?" he asked.

Valentina stood then, because it was the last thing she wanted to do. She could have sat there all night. She could have rung in a new dawn, fencing words with this man and dancing closer and closer to that precipice she could feel looming between them, even if she couldn't quite see it.

She could have pretended she didn't feel every moment of this deep inside her, in places she shouldn't. And then pretend further she didn't know what it meant just because she'd never experienced any of it before outside the pages of a book.

But she did know. And this wasn't her life to ruin. And so she stood, smoothing her hands down her skirt and wishing she hadn't been quite so impetuous in that London bathroom.

If you hadn't been, you wouldn't be here, something in her replied. *Is that what you want?*

And she knew that she didn't. Valentina had a whole life left to live with a man she would call husband who would never know her, not really. She had duty to look forward to, and a lifetime of charity and good works, all of which would be vetted by committees and commented on by the press. She had public adulation and a marriage that would involve the mechanical creation of babies before petering off into a nice friendship, if she was lucky.

Maybe the making of the babies would be fun with her prince. What did she know? All she knew so far was that he didn't do...this. He didn't affect her the way Achilles did, lounging there like hard-packed danger across a conference table, his gaze too dark and the gold in it making her pulse kick at her.

She'd never felt anything like this before. She doubted she'd ever feel it again.

Valentina couldn't quite bring herself to regret it.

But she couldn't stay here tonight and blow up the rest of Natalie's life, either. That would be treating this little gift that she'd been given with nothing but contempt.

"Have I given you leave to go?" Achilles asked, with what she knew was entirely feigned astonishment. "I am clearly confused in some way. I keep thinking you work for me."

She didn't know how he could do that. How he could seem to loom over her when she was the one standing up and looking down at him.

"And because I'd like to continue working for you," Valentina forced herself to say in as measured a tone as she could manage, "I'm going to leave now. We can pick this up in the morning." She tapped the table with one finger. "Pick *this* up, I mean. These contracts and the deal. Not this descent into madness, which I think we can chalk up to exhaustion."

Achilles only watched her for a moment. Those hands that she could picture too easily against her own flesh curled over the armrests of his chair, and her curse was that she imagined she *was* that chair. His legs were thrust out before him, long and lean. His usual suit was slightly rumpled, his tie having been tugged off and tossed aside hours earlier, so she could see the olive skin at his neck and a hint of crisp, black hair. He looked simultaneously sleepy and breathlessly, impossibly lethal—with an intensity that made that hot ache between her legs seem to swallow her whole.

And the look in his eyes made everything inside her draw tight, then pulse harder.

"Do you have a problem with that?" she asked, and she meant to sound impatient. Challenging. But she thought both of them were entirely too aware that what came out instead was rather more plaintive than planned.

As if she was really asking him if he was okay with everything that had happened here tonight. She was clearly too dazed to function.

She needed to get away from him while she still had access to what little of her brain remained in all this smoke and flame.

"Do you require my permission?" Achilles lifted his chin, and his dark eyes glittered. Valentina held her breath. "So far tonight it seems you are laboring under the impression that you give the permission, not me. You make the rules, not me. It is as if I am here for no other purpose than to serve you."

And there was no reason at all that his words, spoken in that soft, if dangerous way, should make her skin prickle. But they did. As if a man like Achilles did not have to issue threats, he was the threat. Why pile a threat on top of the threat? When the look on his face would do.

"I will see you in the morning," Valentina said, resolutely. "When I'll be happy to accept your apology."

Achilles lounged farther down in his chair, and she had the strangest notion that he was holding himself back. Keeping himself in place. Goose bumps shivered to life over her shoulders and down her arms.

His gaze never left hers.

"Go," he said, and there was no pretending it wasn't an order. "But I would not lie awake tonight anticipating the contours of my apology. It will never come."

She wanted to reply to that, but her mouth was too dry and she couldn't seem to move. Not so much as a muscle.

And as if he knew it, Achilles kept going in that same intensely quiet way.

"Tonight when you can't sleep, when you toss and turn and stare up at yet another ceiling I own, I want you to think of all the other reasons you could be wide awake in the small hours of the night. All the things that I could do to you. Or have you do to me. All the thousands of ways I will be imagining us together, just like that, under the same roof."

"That is completely inappropriate, Mr. Casilieris, and I think you know it."

But she knew full well she didn't sound nearly as outraged as she should. And only partially because her voice was a mere whisper.

"Have you never wondered how we would fit? Have

you not tortured herself with images of my possession?" Achilles's hard mouth curved then, a wicked crook in one corner that she knew, somehow, would haunt her. She could feel it deep inside her like its own bright fire. "Tonight, I think, you will."

And Valentina stopped pretending there was any way out of this conversation besides the precise images he'd just mentioned, acted out all over this office. She walked stiffly around the table and gave him a wide, wide berth as she passed.

When she made it to the door of the conference room, she didn't look behind her to see if he was watching. She knew he was. She could feel it.

Fire and lightning, thunder and need.

She ran.

And heard his laughter follow behind her like the leading edge of a storm she had no hope of outwitting, no matter how fast she moved.

CHAPTER FIVE

ACHILLES ORDINARILY ENJOYED his victory parties. Reveled in them, in fact. Not for him any nod toward false humility or any pretense that he didn't deeply enjoy these games of high finance with international stakes. But tonight he couldn't seem to get his head into it, and no matter that he'd been fighting to buy out this particular iconic Manhattan hotel—which he planned to make over in his own image, the blend of European elegance and Greek timelessness that was his calling card in the few hotels scattered across the globe that he'd deemed worthy of the Casilieris name—for nearly eighteen months.

He should have been jubilant. It irritated him—deeply—that he couldn't quite get there.

His group had taken over a New York steak house renowned for its high-end clientele and specialty drinks to match to celebrate the deal he'd finally put through today after all this irritating wrangling. Ordinarily he would allow himself a few drinks to blur out his edges for a change. He would even smile and pretend he was a normal man, like all the rest, made of flesh and blood instead of dollar signs and naked ambition—an improvement by far over the monster he kept locked up tight beneath. Nights like this were his opportunity to pretend to be like anyone else, and Achilles usually indulged that impulse.

He might not have been a normal man—he'd never been a normal man—but it amused him to pretend otherwise every now and again. He was renowned for his surliness as much as his high expectations, but if that was all there was to it—to him—he never would have gotten anywhere in business. It took a little charm to truly manipulate his enemies and his opponents and even his acolytes the way he liked to do. It required that he be as easy telling a joke as he was taking over a company or using his fiercest attorneys to hammer out a deal that served him, and only him, best.

But tonight he was charmless all the way through.

He stood at the bar, nursing a drink he would have much preferred to toss back and follow with a few more of the same, his attention entirely consumed by his princess as she worked the room. As ordered.

"Make yourself useful, please," he'd told her when they'd arrived. "Try to charm these men. If you can."

He'd been deliberately insulting. He'd wanted her to imagine he had some doubt that she could pull such a thing off. He'd wanted her to feel the way he did—grouchy and irritable and outside his own skin.

She made him feel like an adolescent.

But Valentina had not seemed the least bit cowed. Much less insulted—which had only made him feel that much more raw.

"As you wish," she'd murmured in that overly obsequious voice she used when, he thought, she most wanted to get her claws into him. She'd even flashed that bland smile of hers at him, which had its usual effect—making his blood seem too hot for his own veins. "Your slightest desire is my command, of course."

And the truth was, Achilles should have known better. The kind of men he liked to manipulate best, especially when it came to high-stakes deals like the one he'd closed tonight, were not the sort of men he wanted anywhere near his princess. If the real Natalie had been here, she would have disappeared. She would have dispensed her usual round of cool greetings and even cooler congratulations, none of which encouraged anyone to cozy up to her. Then she would have sat in this corner or that, her expression blank and her attention focused entirely on one of her devices. She would have done that remarkable thing she did, that he had never thought to admire as much as perhaps he should have, which was her ability to be both in the room and invisible at the same time.

Princess Valentina, by contrast, couldn't have stayed invisible if her life depended on it. She was the furthest thing from *invisible* that Achilles had ever seen. It was as if the world was cast into darkness and she was its only light, that bright and that impossibly silvery and smooth, like her own brand of moonlight.

She moved from one group to the next, all gracious smiles. And not that bland sort of smile she used entirely too pointedly and too well, which invariably worked his last nerve, but one he'd seen in too many photographs he'd looked at much too late at night. Hunched over his laptop like some kind of obsessed troll while she slept beneath the same roof, unaware, which only made him that much more infuriated.

With her, certainly. But with himself even more.

Tonight she was the consummate hostess, as if this was her victory celebration instead of his. He could hear her airy laugh from across the room, far more potent than another woman's touch. And worse, he could see her. Slender and graceful, inhabiting a pencil skirt and well-cut jacket as if they'd been crafted specifically for her. When he knew perfectly well that those were his assistant's clothes, and they certainly weren't bespoke.

But that was Valentina's power. She made everything in her orbit seem to be only hers. Crafted specifically and especially for her.

Including him, Achilles thought—and he hated it. He was not a man a woman could put on a leash. He'd never given a woman any kind of power over him in his life, and he didn't understand how this creature who was engaged in a full-scale deception—who was running a con on him *even now*—somehow seemed to have the upper hand in a battle he was terribly afraid only he knew they were fighting.

It was unconscionable. It made him want to tear down this building—hell, the whole city—with his bare hands.

Or better yet, put them on her.

All the men around her lapped it up, of course. They stood too close. They put their hands on her elbow, or her shoulder, to emphasize a point that Achilles did not have to hear to know did not require emphasis. And certainly did not require touch.

She was moonlight over this grim, focused life of his, and he had no idea how he was going to make it through a world cast in darkness without her.

If he was appalled by that sentiment—and he was, deeply and wholly—it didn't seem to matter. He couldn't seem to turn it off.

It was far easier to critique her behavior instead.

So Achilles watched. And seethed. He catalogued every single touch, every single laugh, every single time she tilted back her pretty face and let her sleek copper hair fall behind her, catching all the light in the room. He brooded over the men who surrounded her, knowing full well that each and every one of them was imagining her naked. Hell, so was he.

But he was the only person in this room who knew what he was looking at. They thought she was Natalie Monette, his dependable assistant. He was the only one who knew who she really was.

By the time Valentina finished a full circuit of the room, Achilles was in a high, foul temper.

"Are you finished?" he asked when she came to stand by his side again, his tone a dark slap he did nothing at all to temper. "Or will you actually whore yourself out in lieu of dessert?"

He meant that to hurt. He didn't care if he was an ass. He wanted to knock her back a few steps.

But of course Valentina only shot him an arch, amused look, as if she was biting back laughter.

"That isn't very nice," she said simply.

That was all.

And yet Achilles felt that bloom of unfortunate heat inside him all over again, and this time he knew exactly what it was. He didn't like it any better than he had before, and yet there it sat, eating at him from the inside out.

It didn't matter if he told himself he didn't wish to feel shame. All Valentina had to do was look at him as if he was a misbehaving child, tell him he *wasn't being nice* when he'd built an entire life out of being the very opposite of nice and hailing that as the source of his vast power and influence—and there it was. Heavy in him, like a length of hard, cold chain.

How had he given this woman so much power over him? How had he failed to see that was what was happening while he'd imagined he was giving her the rope with which to hang herself?

This could not go on. He could not allow this to go on.

The truth was, Achilles couldn't seem to get a handle on this situation the way he'd planned to when he'd realized who she was on the plane. He'd imagined it would be an amusing sort of game to humble a high and mighty spoiled-rotten princess who had never worked a day in her life and imagined she could deceive *the* Achilles Casilieris so boldly. He'd imagined it would be entertaining—and over swiftly. He supposed he'd imagined he'd be shipping her back to her palace and her princessy life and her proper royal fiancé by the end of the first day.

But Valentina wasn't at all who he'd thought she'd be. If she was spoiled—and she had to be spoiled, by definition, he was certain of it—she hid it. No matter what he threw at her, no matter what he demanded, she simply did it. Not always well, but she did it. She didn't complain. She didn't try to weasel out of any tasks she didn't like. She didn't even make faces or let out those long-suffering sighs that so many of his support staff did when they thought he couldn't hear them.

In fact, Valentina was significantly more cheerful than any other assistant he'd ever had—including Natalie.

She was nothing like perfect, but that made it worse. If she was perfect, maybe he could have dismissed her or ignored her, despite the game she was playing. But he couldn't seem to get her out of his head.

It was that part he couldn't accept. Achilles lived a highly compartmentalized life by design, and he liked it that way. He kept his women in the smallest, most easily controlled and thus ignored space. It had been many, many years since he'd allowed sex to control his thoughts, much less his life. It was only sex, after all. And what was sex to a man who could buy the world if he so chose? It was a release, yes. Enjoyable, even.

But Achilles couldn't remember the last time he'd woken in the night, his heart pounding, the hardest part of him awake and aware. With nothing in his head but her. Yet it was a nightly occurrence since Valentina had walked onto his plane.

It was bordering on obsession.

And Achilles did not get obsessed. He did not *want*.

He did not *need*. He took what interested him and then he forgot about it when the next thing came along.

And he couldn't think of a single good reason why he shouldn't do the same with her.

"Do you have something you wish to say to me?" Valentina asked, her soft, smooth voice snapping him back to this party that bored him. This victory that should have excited him, but that he only found boring now.

"I believe I said it."

"You misunderstand me," she replied, smiling. From a distance it would look as if they were discussing something as light and airy as that curve to her mouth, he thought. Achilles would have been impressed had he not been close enough to see that cool gleam in her green gaze. "I meant your apology. Are you ready to give it?"

He felt his own mouth curve then, in nothing so airy. Or light.

"Do I strike you as a man who apologizes, Miss Monette?" he asked her, making no attempt to ease the steel in his voice. "Have I ever done so in all the time you've known me?"

"A man who cannot apologize is not quite a man, is he, Mr. Casilieris?" This time he thought her smile was meant to take away the sting of her words. To hide the insult a little. Yet it only seemed to make it worse. "I speak philosophically, of course. But surely the only people who can't bring themselves to apologize are those who fear that any admission of guilt or wrongdoing diminishes them. I think we can both agree that's the very opposite of strength."

"You must tell me if I appear diminished, then," he growled at her, and he had the satisfaction of watching that pulse in her neck go wild. "Or weak in some way."

He wasn't surprised when she excused herself and went back to working the crowd. But he was surprised he let her.

Not here, he cautioned that wild thing inside him that he'd never had to contend with before, not over a woman. And never so raw and bold. *Not now*.

Later that night, they sat in his car as it slid through the streets of Manhattan in the midst of a summer thunderstorm, and Achilles cautioned himself not to act rashly.

Again.

But Valentina sat there beside him, staring out the window with a faint smile on her face. She'd settled beside him on the wide, plush seat without a word, as if it hardly mattered to her if he spoke or not. If he berated her, if he ignored her. As if she was all alone in this car or, worse, as if her mind was far away on more interesting topics.

And he couldn't tolerate it.

Achilles could think of nothing but her, she was eating him alive like some kind of impossible acid, yet *her* mind was miles away. She didn't seem to notice or care what she did to him when he was the one who was allowing her grand deception to continue—instead of outing her the way he should have the moment he'd understood who she was.

His hands moved before he knew what he meant to do, as if they had a mind of their own.

He didn't ask. He didn't push or prod at her or fence more words, forcing some sort of temper or explosion that would lead them where he wanted her to go. He didn't stack that deck.

He simply reached across the backseat, wrapped his hand around the back of her neck and hauled her closer to him.

She came easily, as if she really was made of nothing but light. He pulled her until she was sprawled across his lap, one hand braced on his thigh and another at his side. Her body was as lithe and sweetly rounded as he'd imagined it would be, but better. Much, much better. She smelled like a dream, something soft and something sweet, and all of it warm and female and *her*. Valentina.

But all he cared about was the fact that that maddening mouth of hers was close to his.

Finally.

"What are you doing?" she breathed.

"I should think that was obvious," he growled. "And overdue."

And then, at last, he kissed her.

He wasn't gentle. He wasn't anything like tentative. He was neither soft nor kind, because it was too late for that.

He claimed her. Took her. He reminded her who he was with every slick, intense slide of his tongue. Or maybe he was reminding himself.

And he couldn't stop himself once the taste of her exploded inside him, making him reel. He wanted more. He wanted everything.

But she was still fighting him, that stubbornness of hers that made his whole body tight and needy. Not with her body, which was wrapped around him, supple and sweet, in a way that made him feel drunk. Not with her arms, which she'd sneaked around his shoulders as if she needed to hold on to him to keep herself upright.

It was that mouth of hers that had been driving him wild since the start.

He pulled his lips from hers. Then he slid his hands up to take her elegant cheekbones between his palms. He tilted her face where he wanted it, making the angle that much slicker. That much sweeter.

"Kiss me back," he demanded, pulling back farther to scowl at her, all this unaccustomed need making him impatient. And testy.

She looked stunned. And entirely too beautiful. Her green eyes were wide and dazed behind those clear glasses she wore. Her lips were parted, distractingly soft and faintly swollen already.

Achilles was hard and he was greedy and he wanted nothing more than to bury himself inside her here and now, and finally get rid of this obsession that was eating him alive.

Or indulge in it awhile.

"In case you are confused," he told her, his voice still a growl, "that was an order."

She angled herself back, just slightly. As if she was trying to sit up straighter against him. He didn't allow it. He liked her like this. Off balance and under his control, and he didn't much care if that made him a savage. He'd only ever pretended to be anything else, and only occasionally, at that.

"I *am* kissing you back," she said, and there was a certain haughtiness in her voice that delighted him. It made him grin, imagining all the many ways he could make her pay for that high-born, inbred superiority that he wanted to lap up like cream.

"Not well enough," he told her.

Her cheeks looked crisp and red, but she didn't shrink away from him. She didn't so much as blink.

"Maybe we don't have any chemistry," she theorized in that same voice, making it sound as if that was a foregone conclusion. "Not every woman in the world finds you attractive, Mr. Casilieris. Did you ever think of that?"

Achilles pulled her even more off balance, holding her over his lap and in his arms, right where he wanted her.

"No," he said starkly, and he didn't care if his greed and longing was all over his face, revealing more to her than he had ever shared with anyone. Ever. "I don't think either of those things is a problem."

Then he set his mouth to hers, and proved it.

Valentina thought she'd died and gone to a heaven she'd never dreamed of before. Wicked and wild and *better*. So very much better than anything she could have come up with in her most brilliant and dark-edged fantasies.

She had never been truly kissed before—if that was even the word to describe something so dominant and so powerful and so deeply, erotically thrilling—but she had no intention of sharing her level of inexperience with Achilles. Not when he seemed so close to some kind of edge and so hell-bent on taking her with him, toppling over the side into all of this sensation and need.

So she simply mimicked him. When he tilted his head, she did the same. She balled up her hands in his exquisitely soft shirt, up there against the hard planes of his chest tucked beneath his dark suit coat. She was aware of his hard hands on her face. She exulted in his arms like steel, holding her and caging her against him. She lost herself in that desperately cruel mouth as it moved over hers, the touch of his rough jaw, the impossible heat.

God help her, the heat.

And she was aware of that hard ridge beneath her, suddenly. She couldn't seem to keep from wriggling against it. Once, daringly. Then again when she heard that deep, wild and somehow savagely beautiful male noise he made in response.

And Valentina forgot about her vows, old and forthcoming. She forgot about faraway kingdoms and palaces and the life she'd lived there. She forgot about the promises she'd made and the ones that had been made in her name, because all of that seemed insubstantial next to the sheer, overwhelming wonder of Achilles Casilieris kissing her like a man possessed in the back of his town car.

This was her holiday. Her little escape. This was nothing but a dream, and he was, too. A fantasy of the life she might have lived had she been anyone else. Had she ever been anything like normal.

She forgot where they were. She forgot the role she was supposed to be playing. There was nothing in all the world but Achilles and the wildness he summoned up with every drag of his mouth against hers.

The car moved beneath them, but all Valentina could focus on was him. That hot possession of his mouth. The fire inside her.

And the lightning that she knew was his, the thunder storming through her, teaching her that she knew less about her body than he did. Much, much less. When he shifted so he could rub his chest against hers, she understood that he knew her nipples had pebbled into hard little points. When he laughed slightly as he rearranged her arms around his shoulders, she understood that he knew all her limbs were weighted down with the force of that greedy longing coursing through her veins.

The more he kissed her, over and over again as if time had no meaning and he could do this forever, she understood that he knew everything.

When he pulled his mouth from hers again, Valentina heard a soft, whimpering sound of protest. It took her one shuddering beat of her heart, then another, to realize she'd made it.

She couldn't process that. It was so abandoned, so thoughtless and wild—how could that be her?

"If we do not get out of this car right now," Achilles told her, his gaze a dark and breathtaking gold that slammed into her and lit her insides on fire, "we will not get out of it for some time. Not until I've had my fill of you. Is that how you want our first time to go, *glikia mou*? In the backseat of a car?"

For a moment Valentina didn't know what he meant.

One hastily sucked-in breath later, she realized the car had come to a stop outside Achilles's building. Her cheeks flushed with a bright heat, but worse, she knew that he could see it. He saw everything—hadn't she just realized the truth of that? He watched her as she flushed, and he liked it. That deeply male curve in the corner of his mouth made that plain.

Valentina struggled to free herself from his hold then, to climb off his lap and sit back on the seat herself, and she was all too aware that he let her.

She didn't focus on that. She couldn't. That offhanded show of his innate strength made her feel… slippery, inside and outside and high between her legs. She tossed herself off his lap, her gaze tangling with his in a way that made the whole world seem to spin a little, and then she threw herself out the door. She summoned a smile from somewhere and aimed it at the doormen.

Breathe, she ordered herself. *Just breathe.*

Because she couldn't do this. This wasn't who she was. She hadn't held on to her virginity all this time to toss it aside at the very first temptation…had she?

This couldn't be who she was. It couldn't.

She'd spent her whole life practicing how to appear unruffled and serene under any and all circumstances, though she couldn't recall ever putting it to this kind of test before. She made herself breathe. She made herself smile. She sank into the familiarity of her public persona, wielding it like that armor she'd wanted, because it occurred to her it was the toughest and most resilient armor she had.

Achilles followed her into that bright and shiny elevator in the back of the gleaming lobby, using his key to close the doors behind them. He did not appear to notice or care that she was newly armored, especially while he seemed perfectly content to look so...disreputable.

His suit jacket hung open, and she was sure it had to be obvious to even the most casual observer that she'd had her hands all over his chest and his shirt. And she found it was difficult to think of that hard mouth of his as cruel now that she knew how it tasted. More, how it felt on hers, demanding and intense and—

Stop, she ordered herself. *Now.*

He leaned back against the wall as the elevator started to move, his dark gold eyes hooded and intent when they met hers. He didn't say a word. Maybe he didn't have to. Her heart was pounding so loud that Valentina was certain it would have drowned him out if he'd shouted.

But Achilles did not shout.

On the contrary, when the elevator doors shut behind them, securing them in his penthouse, he only continued to watch her in that same intense way. She moved into the great living room, aware that he followed her, silent and faintly lazy.

It made her nervous. That was what she told herself that fluttery feeling was, lodged there beneath her ribs. And lower, if she was honest. Much lower.

"I'm going to bed," she said. And then instantly

wished she'd phrased that differently when she heard it echo there between them, seeming to fill up the cavernous space, beating as madly within her as her own frenzied heart. "Alone."

Achilles gave the impression of smiling without actually doing so. He thrust his hands into the pockets of his dark suit and regarded her solemnly, save for that glittering thing in his dark gaze.

"If that is what you wish, *glikia mou*."

And that was the thing. It wasn't what she wished. It wasn't what she wanted, and especially not when he called her that Greek name that she thought meant *my sweet*. It made her want to taste that word on that mouth of his. It made her want to find out exactly how sweet he thought she was.

It made her want to really, truly be someone else so she could do all the things that trampled through her head, making her chest feel tight while the rest of her...yearned.

Her whole life had been an exercise in virtue and duty, and she'd thought that meant something. She'd thought that *said* something about who she was. Valentina had been convinced that she'd held on to her chastity all this time, long after everyone she'd known had rid themselves of theirs, as a gift to her future.

But the night all around her told her something different. It had stripped away all the lies she'd told herself—or Achilles had. All the places she'd run and hid across all these years. Because the truth was that she'd never been tested. Was it truly virtue if she'd never been the least bit tempted to give it away? Or was it only coincidence that she'd never encountered anything that had felt the least bit compelling in that regard? Was it really holding on to something if she'd never felt the least bit like getting rid of it?

Because everything tonight was different. Valentina was different—or, worse, she thought as she stared at Achilles across the little bit of space that separated them, she had never been who she'd imagined she was. She had never understood that it was possible that a body could drown out what the mind knew to be prudent.

Until now.

She had judged passion all her life and told herself it was a story that weak people told themselves and others to make their sins seem more interesting. More complicated and unavoidable. But the truth was, Valentina had never experienced passion in her life.

Not until Achilles.

"I am your assistant," she told him. Or perhaps she was telling herself. "This must never happen again. If it does, I can't work for you."

"I have already told you that I am more than happy to accommodate—"

"There will be no lateral moves," she threw at him, appalled to hear her voice shaking. "You might lie awake at night imagining what that means and what it would look like, but I don't. I won't."

"Liar."

If he had hauled off and hit her, Valentina didn't think she could have been any more surprised. Shocked. No one had ever called her a liar before, not in all her life.

Then again, chimed in a small voice deep inside, *you never used to lie, did you? Not to others and not to yourself.*

"I have no doubt that you enjoy doing as you please," she spat at him, horrified that any of this was happening and, worse, that she'd let it—when Valentina knew who she was and what she'd be going back to in a few short weeks. "No matter the consequences. But not everyone is as reckless as you."

Achilles didn't quite smirk. "And that is why one of us is a billionaire and the other is his assistant."

"And if we were having a discussion about how to make money," Valentina said from between her teeth, no sign of her trademark serenity, "I would take your advice—but this is my life."

Guilt swamped her as she said that. Because, of course, it wasn't her life. It was Natalie's. And she had the sick feeling that she had already complicated it beyond the point of return. It didn't matter that Natalie had texted her to say that she'd kissed Prince Rodolfo, far away in Murin and neck-deep in Valentina's real life, however little Valentina had thought about it since she'd left it behind. Valentina was going to marry Rodolfo. That her double had kissed him, the way Valentina probably should have, wasn't completely out of line.

But this… This thing she was doing… It was unacceptable on every level. She knew that.

Maybe Natalie has this same kind of chemistry with Rodolfo, something in her suggested. *Maybe he was engaged to the wrong twin.*

Which meant, she knew—because she was that

self-serving—that maybe the wrong twin had been working for Achilles all this time and all of this was inevitable.

She wasn't sure she believed that. But she couldn't seem to stop herself. Or worse, convince herself that she should.

Achilles was still watching her too closely. Once again, she had the strangest notion that he knew too much. That he could see too far inside her.

Don't be silly, she snapped at herself then. *Of course he can't. You're just looking for more ways to feel guilty.*

Because whatever else happened, there was no way Achilles Casilieris would allow the sort of deception Valentina was neck-deep in to take place under his nose if he knew about it. She was certain of that, if nothing else.

"This is what I know about life," Achilles said, his voice a silken thread in the quiet of the penthouse, and Valentina had to repress a little shiver that threatened to shake her spine apart. "You must live it. If all you do is wall yourself off, hide yourself away, what do you have at the end but wasted time?"

Her throat was dry and much too tight. "I would take your advice more seriously if I didn't know you had an ulterior motive."

"I don't believe in wasting time or in ulterior motives," he growled back at her. "And not because I want a taste of you, though I do. And I intend to have it, *glikia mou*, make no mistake. But because you have put yourself on hold. Do you think I can't see it?"

She thought she had to be reeling then. Nothing was solid. She couldn't help but put her hand out, steadying herself on the back of the nearest chair—though it didn't seem to help.

And Achilles was watching her much too closely, with far too much of that disconcerting awareness making his dark gaze shine. "Or is it that you don't know yourself?"

When she was Princess Valentina of Murin, known to the world before her birth. Her life plotted out in its every detail. Her name literally etched in stone into the foundations of the castle where her family had ruled for generations. She had never had the opportunity to lose herself. Not in a dramatic adolescence. Not in her early twenties. She had never been beside herself at some crossroads, desperate to figure out the right path—because there had only ever been one path and she had always known exactly how to walk it, every step of the way.

"You don't know me at all," she told him, trying to sound less thrown and more outraged at the very suggestion that she was any kind of mystery to herself. She'd never had that option. "You're my employer, not my confidant. You know what I choose to show you and nothing more."

"But what you choose to show, and how you choose to show it, tells me exactly who you are." Achilles shook his head, and it seemed to Valentina that he moved closer to her when she could see he didn't. That he was exactly where he'd always been—it was just that he seemed to take over the whole world. She wasn't sure he even tried; he just did. "Or did you imagine I achieved all that I've achieved without managing to read people? Surely you cannot be so foolish."

"I was about to do something deeply foolish," she said tightly. And not exactly smartly. "But I've since come to my senses."

"No one is keeping you here." His hands were thrust deep into his pockets, and he stood where he'd stopped, a few steps into the living room from those elevator doors. His gaze was all over her, but nothing else was touching her. He wasn't even blocking her escape route back to the guest room on this floor.

And she understood then. He was giving her choice. He was putting it on her. He wasn't simply sweeping her off into all that wild sensation—when he must have known he could have. He easily could have. If he hadn't stopped in the car, what would they be doing now?

But Valentina already knew the answer to that. She could feel her surrender inside her like heat.

And she thought she hated him for it.

Or should.

"I'm going to sleep," she said. She wanted her voice to be fierce. Some kind of condemnation. But she thought she sounded more determined than resolved. "I will see you in the morning. Sir."

Achilles smiled. "I think we both know you will see me long before that. And in your dreams, *glikia mou*, I doubt I will be so chivalrous."

Valentina pressed her lips tight together and did not allow herself to respond to him. Especially because she wanted to so very, very badly—and she knew, somehow, that it would lead nowhere good. It couldn't.

Instead, she turned and headed for her room. It was an unremarkable guest room appropriate for staff, but the best thing about it was the lock on the door. Not that she thought he would try to get in.

She was far more concerned that she was the one who would try to get out.

"One of these days," he said from behind her, his voice low and intense, "you will stop running. It is a foregone conclusion, I am afraid. And then what?"

Valentina didn't say a word. But she didn't have to.

When she finally made it to her room and threw the dead bolt behind her, the sound of it echoed through the whole of the penthouse like a gong, answering Achilles eloquently without her having to open her mouth.

Telling him exactly how much of a coward she was, in case he hadn't already guessed.

CHAPTER SIX

IN THE DAYS that followed that strange night and Achilles's world-altering kiss that had left her raw and aching and wondering if she'd ever feel like herself again, Valentina found she couldn't bear the notion that she was twenty-seven years old and somehow a stranger to herself.

Her future was set in stone. She'd always known that. And she'd never fought against all that inevitability because what was the point? She could fight as much as she wanted and she'd still be Princess Valentina of Murin, only with a stain next to her name. That had always seemed to her like the very definition of futility.

But in the days that followed that kiss, it occurred to her that perhaps it wasn't the future she needed to worry about, but her past. She hadn't really allowed herself to think too closely about what it meant that Natalie had been raised by the woman who was very likely Valentina's own mother. Because, of course, there was no other explanation for the fact she and Natalie looked so much alike. Identical twins couldn't just randomly occur, and certainly not when one of them was a royal. There were too many people watching royal births too closely. Valentina had accepted the story that her mother had abandoned her, because it had always been couched in terms of Frederica's mental illness. Valentina had imagined her mother living out her days in some or other institution somewhere, protected from harm.

But the existence of Natalie suggested that Frederica was instead a completely different person from the one Valentina had imagined all this time. The woman who now called herself Erica had clearly not wasted away in a mental institution, all soothing pastels and injections and no ability to contact her own child. On the contrary, this Erica had lived a complicated life after her time in the palace that had nothing to do with any hospital—and though she'd clearly had two daughters, she'd taken only one with her when she'd gone.

Valentina didn't entirely understand how she could be quite so hurt by a betrayal that had happened so long ago and that she hadn't known about until recently. She didn't understand why it mattered so much to her. But the more she tried to tell herself that it was silly to be so bothered, the more bothered she got.

It was only when she had gone round and round and round on that almost too many times to count that Valentina accepted the fact she was going to have to do something about it.

And all these years, she'd never known how to go about looking for her mother even if she'd wanted to. She would have had to ask her father directly, the very idea of which made her shudder—even now, across an ocean or two from his throne and his great reserve and his obvious reluctance to discuss Frederica at all. Barring that, she would have had to speak to one of the high-level palace aides whose role was to serve her father in every possible way and who therefore had access to most of the family secrets. She doubted somehow that they would have told her all the things that she wanted to know—or even a few of them. And they certainly would have run any questions she had past her father first, which would have defeated the purpose of asking them.

Valentina tried to tell herself that was why she'd never asked.

But now she was tucked up in a lethally dangerous billionaire's penthouse in New York City, away from all the palace intrigue and protocol, and far too aware of the things a man like Achilles could do with only a kiss. To say nothing of his businesses. What was an old family secret to a man like Achilles?

And even though in many ways she had fewer resources at her fingertips and fewer people to ask for ancient stories and explanations, in the end, it was very simple. Because Valentina had Natalie's mobile, which had to mean she had direct access to her own story. If she dared look for it.

The Valentina who had seen her own mirror image in a bathroom in London might not have dared. But the Valentina who had lost herself in the raw fire of Achilles's kiss, on the other hand, dared all manner of things.

It was that Valentina who opened up Natalie's list of

contacts, sitting there in her locked bedroom in Achilles's penthouse. She scrolled down, looking for an entry that read *Mom*. Or *Mum*. Or any variation of *Mother* she could think of.

But there was nothing.

That stymied her, but she was aware enough to realize that the sensation deep in her belly was not regret. It was relief. As if, in the end, she preferred these mysteries to what was likely to be a vicious little slap of truth.

You are such a coward, she told herself.

Because it wasn't as if her father—or Valentina herself, for that matter—had ever been in hiding. The truth was that her mother could have located her at any point over these last twenty-seven years. That she hadn't done so told Valentina all she needed to know about Frederica's maternal feelings, surely.

Well. What she *needed* to know perhaps, but there was a great deal more she *wanted* to know, and that was the trouble.

She kept scrolling until she found an entry marked *Erica*. She thought that told her a great deal about Natalie's relationship with this woman who was likely mother to them both. It spoke of a kind of distance that Valentina had certainly never contemplated when she'd thought about her own mother from time to time over the past nearly thirty years. In her head, of course, any reunion with the woman she'd imagined had been locked away in a pleasantly secure institution would be filled with love. Regret. Soft, sweet arms wrapped around her, and a thousand apologies for somehow managing to abandon and then never find her way back to a baby who lived at one of the most famous addresses in the world.

She wasn't entirely sure why the simple fact of the woman's first name in a list of contacts made it so clear that all of that was a lie. Not just a harmless fantasy to make a motherless child feel better about her fate, but something infinitely more dangerous, somehow.

Valentina wanted to shut down the mobile phone. She wanted to throw it across the small room and pretend that she'd never started down this road in the first place.

But it occurred to her that possibly, she was trying to talk herself out of doing this thing she was certain she needed to do.

Because Achilles might have imagined that he could see these mysteries in her, but what scared Valentina was that she could, too. That he'd identified a terrible weakness in her, and that meant anyone could.

Perhaps she wasn't who she thought she was. Perhaps she never had been. Perhaps, all this time, she'd imagined she'd been walking down a set path when she hadn't.

If she was honest, the very idea made her want to cry.

It had been important, she thought then, sitting cross-legged on the bed with the summer light streaming in from the windows—crucially important, even—to carry on the morning after that kiss as if nothing had changed. Because she had to pretend that nothing had. That she didn't know too much now. That she didn't think of that kiss every time she looked at Achilles. She'd gone to work, and she'd done her job, and she'd stayed as much in his presence as she ever did—and she thought that she deserved some kind of award for the acting she'd done. So cool, so composed.

So utterly unbothered by the fact she now knew how he tasted.

And she tried to convince herself that only she knew that she was absolutely full of it.

But one day bled into the next, and she'd found that her act became harder and harder to pull off, instead of easier. She couldn't understand it. It wasn't as if Achilles was doing anything, necessarily. He was Achilles, of course. There was always that look in his eyes, as if he was but waiting for her to give him a sign.

Any sign.

As if, were she to do so, he would drop everything he was doing—no matter where they were and what was happening around them—and sweep them right back into that storm of sensation that she found simmered inside her, waiting. Just waiting.

Just as he was.

It was the notion that she was the one who held the power—who could make all of that happen with a simple word or glance—that she found kept her up at night. It made her shake. It polluted her dreams and made her drift off entirely too many times while she was awake, only to be slapped back down to earth when Achilles's voice turned silken, as if he knew.

Somehow, this all made her determined to seek out the one part of her life that had never made sense, and had never fit in neatly into the tidy narrative she'd believed all her life and knew back and forth.

Today was a rare afternoon when Achilles had announced that he had no need of her assistance while he tended to his fitness in his personal gym because, he'd gritted at her, he needed to clear his head. Valentina had repaired to her bedroom to work out a few snarls in his schedule and return several calls from the usual people wanting advice on how to approach him with various bits of news he was expected to dislike intensely. She'd changed out of Natalie's usual work uniform and had gratefully pulled on a pair of jeans and a T-shirt, feeling wildly rebellious as she did so. And then a little bit embarrassed that her life was clearly so staid and old-fashioned that she found denim a personal revolution.

Many modern princesses dressed casually at times, she was well aware. Just as she was even more aware that none of them were related to her father, with his antiquated notions of propriety. And therefore none of them would have to suffer his disapproval should she find herself photographed looking "common" despite her ancient bloodline.

But she wasn't Princess Valentina here in New York, where no one cared what she wore. And maybe that was why Valentina pulled the trigger. She didn't cold-call the number that she'd found on her sister's phone—and there was something hard and painful in her chest even thinking that word, *sister*. She fed the number into a little piece of software that one of Achilles's companies had been working on, and she let it present her with information that she supposed she should have had some sort of scruple about using. But she didn't.

Valentina imagined that said something about her, too, but she couldn't quite bring herself to care about that the way she thought she ought to have.

In a push of a button, she had a billing address. Though the phone number itself was tied to the area code of a far-off city, the billing address was right here in Manhattan.

It was difficult not see that as some kind of sign.

Valentina slipped out of the penthouse then, without giving herself time to second-guess what she was about to do. She smiled her way through the lobby the way she always did, and then she set out into New York City by herself.

All by herself.

No guards. No security. Not even Achilles's brooding presence at her side. She simply walked. She made her way through the green, bright stretch of Central Park, headed toward the east side and the address Achilles's software had provided. No one spoke to her. No one called her name. No cameras snapped at her, recording her every move.

After a while, Valentina stopped paying attention to the expression on her face. She stopped worrying about her posture and whether or not her hair looked unkempt as the faint breeze teased at it. She simply…walked.

Her shoulders seemed to slip down an extra inch or two from her ears. She found herself breathing deeper, taking in the people she passed without analyzing them—without assuming they wanted something from her or were looking to photograph her supposedly "at large" in the world.

About halfway across the park it occurred to her that she'd never felt this way in her life. Alone. Free. Better yet, anonymous. She could have been anybody on the streets. There were locals all over the paths in the park, walking and talking and taking in the summer afternoon as if that was a perfectly normal pastime. To be out on their own, no one the wiser, doing exactly as they pleased.

Valentina realized that whatever happened next, this was the normal she'd spent her life looking for and dreaming about. This exact moment, walking across Central Park while summer made its cheerful noises all around her, completely and entirely on her own.

Freedom, it turned out, made her heart beat a little too fast and too hard inside her chest.

Once she made it to the east side, she headed a little bit uptown, then farther east until she found the address that had been on that billing statement. It looked like all the other buildings on the same block, not exactly dripping in luxury, but certainly no hovel. It was difficult for Valentina to determine the difference between kinds of dwellings in a place like this. Apartment buildings, huge blocks of too many people living on top of each other by choice, seemed strange to her on the face of it. But who was she to determine the difference between prosperous New Yorkers and regular ones? She had lived in a palace all her life. And she suspected that Achilles's sprawling penthouse wasn't a far cry from a palace itself, come to that.

But once she'd located the building she wanted and its dark green awning marked with white scrollwork, she didn't know what to do. Except wait there. As if she was some kind of daring sleuth, just like in the books she'd read as a little girl, when she was just… that same old motherless child, looking for a better story to tell herself.

She chided herself for that instantly. It felt defeating. Despairing. She was anonymous and free and unremarkable, standing on a city street. Nobody in the entire world knew where she was. Nobody would know where to look and nobody was likely to find her if they tried. Valentina couldn't decide if that notion made her feel small and fragile, or vast and powerful. Maybe both at the same time.

She didn't know how long she stood there. She ignored the first few calls that buzzed at her from Natalie's mobile tucked in her pocket, but then realized that standing about speaking on her phone gave her far more of a reason to be out there in the street. Instead of simply standing there doing nothing, looking like she was doing exactly what she was doing, which was looming around as she waited for somebody to turn up.

So she did her job, out there on the street. Or Natalie's job, anyway. She fielded the usual phone calls from the office and, if she was honest, liked the fact that she had somewhere to put all her nervous energy. She was half-afraid that Achilles would call and demand that she return to his side immediately, but she suspected that she was less afraid of that happening than she was hoping that it would, so she didn't have to follow this through.

Because even now, there was a part of her that simply wanted to retreat back into what she already knew. What she'd spent her life believing.

Afternoon was bleeding into evening, and Valentina was beginning to think that she'd completely outstayed her welcome. That Erica was in one of the other places she sometimes stayed, like the one in the Caribbean Natalie had mentioned in a text. That at any moment now it was likely that one of the doormen in the surrounding buildings would call the police to make her move along at last. That they hadn't so far she regarded as some kind of miracle. She finished up the last of the calls she'd been fielding, and told herself that it had been foolish to imagine that she could simply turn up one afternoon, stand around and solve the mysteries of her childhood so easily.

But that was when she saw her.

And Valentina didn't know exactly what it was that had caught her eye. The hair was wrong, not long and coppery like her daughters' but short. Dark. And it wasn't as if Valentina had any memories of this woman, but still. There was something in the way she moved. The way she came down the block, walking quickly, a plastic bag hanging from one wrist and the other hand holding a phone to her ear.

But Valentina knew her. She knew that walk. She knew the gait and the way the woman cocked her head toward the hand holding her phone. She knew the way this woman carried herself.

She recognized her, in other words, when she shouldn't have. When, she realized, despite the fact she'd spent a whole summer afternoon waiting for this moment—she really didn't want to recognize her.

And she'd been nursing fantasies this whole time, little as she wanted to admit that, even to herself. She'd told herself all the things that she would do if this woman appeared. She'd worked out scenarios in her head.

Do you know who I am? she would ask, or demand, and this woman she had always thought of as Federica, but who went by a completely different name—the better to hide, Valentina assumed—would… Cry? Flail about? Offer excuses? She hadn't been able to decide which version she would prefer no matter how many times she'd played it out in her head.

And as this woman who was almost certainly her mother walked toward her, not looking closely enough to see that there was anyone standing down the block a ways in front of her, much less someone who she should have assumed was the daughter she knew as Natalie, Valentina realized what she should have known already. Or maybe, deep down, she had known it—she just hadn't really wanted to admit it.

There was nothing this woman could do to fix anything or change anything or even make it better. She couldn't go back in time. She couldn't change the past. She couldn't choose Valentina instead of Natalie, if that had been the choice she'd made. Valentina wasn't even certain that was something she'd want, if she could go back in time herself, but the fact of the matter was that there was nothing to be done about it now.

And her heart beat at her and beat at her, until she

thought it might beat its way straight out through her ribs, and even as it did, Valentina couldn't pretend that she didn't know that what she was feeling was grief.

Grief, thick and choking. Dark and muddy and deep.

For the childhood she'd never had, and hadn't known she'd missed until now. For the life she might have known had this woman been different. Had Valentina been different. Had her father, perhaps, not been King Geoffrey of Murin. It was all speculation, of course. It was that tearing thing in her belly and that weight on her chest, and that thick, deep mud she worried she might never find her way out of again.

And when Erica drew close to her building's green awning, coming closer to Valentina than she'd been in twenty-seven years, Valentina…said nothing. She let her hair fall forward to cover her face where she leaned against the brick wall. She pretended she was on a serious phone call while the woman who was definitely her mother—of course she was her mother; how had Valentina been tricking herself into pretending she could be anything but that?—turned into the building that Valentina had been staking out all afternoon, and was swallowed up into her own lobby.

For long moments, Valentina couldn't breathe. She wasn't sure she could think.

It was as if she didn't know who she was.

She found herself walking. She lost herself in the tumult of this sprawling mess of a bright and brash city, the noise of car horns in the street, and the blasts of conversation and laughter from the groups of strangers she passed. She made her way back to the park and wandered there as the summer afternoon took on that glassy blue that meant the hour was growing late.

She didn't cry. She hardly saw in front of her. She simply walked.

And dusk was beginning to steal in at last, making the long blocks cold in the long shadows, when she finally made it back to Achilles's building.

One of the doormen brought her up in the elevator, smiling at her as she stepped off. It made her think that perhaps she had smiled in return, though she couldn't tell. It was as if her body was not her own and her face was no longer under her control. She walked into Achilles's grand living room, and stood there. It was as if she still didn't know where she was. As if she still couldn't see. And the huge windows that let Manhattan in all around her only seemed to make her sense of dislocation worse.

"Where the hell have you been?"

That low growl came from above her. Valentina didn't have to turn and look to know that it was Achilles from on high, standing at the top of the stairs that led to his sprawling master suite.

She looked up anyway. Because somehow, the most dangerous man she'd ever met felt like an anchor.

He looked as if he'd just showered. He wore a T-shirt she could tell was soft from down two flights, stretched over his remarkable chest as if it was as enamored of him as she feared she was. Loose black trousers were slung low on his hips, and she had the giddy sense that if he did something like stretch, or breathe too heavily, she would be able to see a swathe of olive skin between the waistband and the hem of his T-shirt.

And suddenly, she wanted nothing more than to see exactly that. More than she could remember wanting anything else. Ever.

"Careful, *glikia mou*, or I will take you up on that invitation written all over your face," Achilles growled as if he was irritated…but she knew better.

Because he knew. He always knew. He could read her when no one else ever had. The masks she wore like they were second nature and the things she pretended for the whole of the rest of the world fooled everybody, but never him.

Never, ever him.

As if there was a real Valentina buried beneath the exterior she'd thought for years was the totality of who she was, and Achilles was the only one who had ever met her. Ever seen her. Ever suspected she existed and then found her, again and again, no matter how hard Valentina worked to keep her hidden away.

Her throat was dry. Her tongue felt as if it no longer fit in her own mouth.

But she couldn't bring herself to look away from him.

She thought about her mother and she thought about her childhood. She thought about the pride she'd taken in that virtue of hers that she'd clung to so fiercely all these years. Or perhaps not so fiercely, as it had been so untested. Was that virtue at all, she wondered?

Or was this virtue?

She had spent all of this time trying to differentiate herself from a woman she thought she knew, but who it turned out she didn't know at all. And for what? She was already trapped in the same life that her mother had abandoned.

Valentina was the one who hadn't left her father. She was the one who had prided herself on being perfect. She was the one who was decidedly not mentally ill, never too overwrought to do the job required of her by her blood and her father's expectations, nothing but a credit to her father in all ways. And she'd reveled in it.

More than reveled in it. It had become the cornerstone of her own self-definition.

And all of it was built on lies. The ones she told herself, and more than that, the lies that had been told to her for her entire life. By everyone.

All Valentina could think as she gazed up the stairs to the man she was only pretending was her employer was that she was done with lies. She wanted something honest. Even—especially—if it was raw.

And she didn't much care if there were consequences to that.

"You say that is if it is a threat," she said quietly. Distinctly. "Perhaps you should rethink your own version of an invitation before it gets you in trouble." She raised her brows in challenge, and knew it. Reveled in it, too. "Sir."

And when Achilles smiled then, it was with sheer masculine triumph, and everything changed.

He had thought she'd left him.

When Achilles had come out of the hard, brutal workout he'd subjected himself to that had done absolutely nothing to make his vicious need for her settle, Achilles had found her gone.

And he'd assumed that was it. The princess had finally had enough. She'd finished playing this downmarket game of hers and gone back to her palaces and her ball gowns and her resplendent little prince who waited for her across the seas.

He'd told himself it was for the best.

He was a man who took things for a living and made an empire out of his conquests, and he had no business whatsoever putting his commoner's hands all over a woman of her pedigree. No business doing it, and worse, he shouldn't want to.

And maybe that was why he found himself on his treadmill again while he was still sucking air from his first workout, running as if every demon he'd vanquished in his time was chasing him all over again, and gaining. Maybe that was why he'd run until he'd thought his lungs might burst, his head might explode or his knees might give out beneath him.

Then he'd run more. And even when he'd exhausted himself all over again, even when he was standing in his own shower with his head bent toward the wall as if she'd bested him personally, it hadn't helped.

The fact of the matter was that he had a taste of Valentina, and nothing else would do.

And what enraged him the most, he'd found—aside from the fact he hadn't had her the way he'd wanted her—was that he'd let her think she'd tricked him all this time. That she would go back behind her fancy gates and her moats and whatever the hell else she had in that palace of hers that he'd looked up online and thought looked exactly like the sort of fairy tale he disdained, and she would believe that she'd played him for a fool.

Achilles thought that might actually eat him alive.

And now here she stood when he thought he'd lost her. At the bottom of his stairs, looking up at him, her eyes dark with some emotion he couldn't begin to define.

But he didn't want to define it. He didn't want to talk about her feelings, and he'd die before he admitted his own, and what did any of that matter anyway? She was here and he was here, and a summer night was creeping in outside.

And the only thing he wanted to think about was sating himself on her at last.

At last and for as long as he could.

Achilles was hardly aware of moving down the stairs even as he did it.

One moment he was at the top, staring down at Valentina's upturned face with her direct challenge ringing in him like a bell, and the next he was upon her. And she was so beautiful. So exquisitely, ruinously beautiful. He couldn't seem to get past that. It was as if it wound around him and through him, changing him, making him new each time he beheld her.

He told himself he hated it, but he didn't look away.

"There is no going back," he told her sternly. "There will be no pretending this didn't happen."

Her smile was entirely too graceful and the look in her green eyes too merry by far. "Do you get that often?"

Achilles felt like a savage. An animal. Too much like that monster he kept down deep inside. And yet he didn't have it in him to mind. He reached out and indulged himself at last while his blood hammered through his veins, running his fingers over that elegant cheekbone of hers, and that single freckle that marred the perfection of her face—and somehow made her all the more beautiful.

"So many jokes," he murmured, not sure how much of the gruffness in his voice was need and how much was that thing like temper that held him fast and fierce. "Everything is so hilarious, suddenly. How much longer do you think you will be laughing, *glikia mou*?"

"I think that is up to you," Valentina replied smoothly, and she was still smiling at him in that same way, graceful and knowing. "Is that why you require so much legal documentation before you take a woman to bed? Do you make them all laugh so much that you fear your reputation as a grumpy icon would take a hit if it got out?"

It was a mark of how far gone he was that he found that amusing. If anyone else had dreamed of saying such a thing to him, he would have lost his sense of humor completely.

He felt his mouth curve. "There is only one way to find out."

And Achilles had no idea what she might do next. He wondered if that was what it was about her, if that was why this thirst for her never seemed to ebb. She was so very different from all the women he'd known before. She was completely unpredictable. He hardly knew, from one moment to the next, what she might do next.

It should have irritated him, he thought. But instead it only made him want her more.

Everything, it seemed, made him want her more. He hadn't realized until now how pale and insubstantial his desires had been before. How little he'd wanted anything.

"There is something I must tell you." She pulled her bottom lip between her teeth after she said that, a little breathlessly, and everything in him stilled.

This was it, he thought. And Achilles didn't know if he was proud of her or sad, somehow, that this great charade was at an end. For surely that was what she planned to tell him. Surely she planned to come clean about who she really was.

And while there was a part of him that wanted to deny that what swirled between them was anything more than sex, simple and elemental, there was a far greater part of him that roared its approval that she should think it was right to identify herself before they went any further.

"You can tell me anything," he told her, perhaps more fiercely than he should. "But I don't know why you imagine I don't already know."

He was fascinated when her cheeks bloomed with that crisp, bright red that he liked a little too much. More each time he saw it, because he liked his princess a little flustered. A little off balance.

But something in him turned over, some foreboding perhaps. Because he couldn't quite imagine why it was that she should be *embarrassed* by the deception she'd practiced on him. He could think of many things he'd like her to feel for attempting to pull something like that over on him, and he had quite a few ideas about how she should pay for that, but embarrassment wasn't quite it.

"I thought you might know," she whispered. "I hope it doesn't matter."

"Everything matters or nothing does, *glikia mou*."

He shifted so he was closer to her. He wanted to care about whatever it was she was about to tell him, but he found the demands of his body were far too loud and too imperative to ignore. He put his hands on her, curling his fingers over her delicate shoulders and then losing himself in their suppleness. And in the delicate line of her arms. And in the sweet feel of her bare skin beneath his palms as he ran them down from her shoulders to her wrists, then back again.

And he found he didn't really care what she planned to confess to him. How could it matter when he was touching her like this?

"I do not require your confession," he told her roughly. "I am not your priest."

If anything, her cheeks flared brighter.

"I'm a virgin," she blurted out, as if she had to force herself to say it.

For a moment, it was as if she'd struck him. As if she'd picked up one of the sculptures his interior designer had littered about his living room and clobbered him with it.

"I beg your pardon?"

But she was steadier then. "You heard me. I'm a virgin. I thought you knew." She swallowed, visibly, but she didn't look away from him. "Especially when I didn't know how to kiss you."

Achilles didn't know what to do with that.

Or rather, he knew exactly what to do with it, but was afraid that if he tossed his head back and let himself go the way he wanted to—roaring out his primitive take on her completely unexpected confession to the rafters—it might terrify her.

And the last thing in the world he wanted to do was terrify her.

He knew he should care that this wasn't quite the confession he'd expected. That as far as he could tell, Valentina had no intention of telling him who she was. Ever. He knew that it should bother him, and perhaps on some level it did, but the only thing he could seem to focus on was the fact that she was untouched.

Untouched.

He was the only man in all the world who had ever tasted her. Touched her. Made her shiver, and catch her breath, and moan. That archaic word seemed to beat in place of his heart.

Virgin. Virgin. Virgin.

Until it was as if he knew nothing but that. As if her innocence shimmered between them, beckoning and sweet, and she was his for the taking.

And, oh, how Achilles liked to take the things he wanted.

"Are you sure you wish to waste such a precious gift on the likes of me?" he asked, and he heard the stark greed beneath the laziness he forced into his tone. He heard exactly how much he wanted her. He was surprised it didn't seem to scare her the way he thought it should. "After all, there is nothing particularly special about me. I have money, that's all. And as you have reminded me, I am your boss. The ethical considerations are legion."

He didn't know why he said that. Any of that. Was it to encourage her to confess her real identity to him? Was it to remind her of the role she'd chosen to play— although not today, perhaps?

Or was it to remind him?

Either way, she only lifted her chin. "You don't have to take it," she said, as if it was of no import to her one way or the other. "Certainly not if you have some objection."

She lifted one shoulder, then dropped it, and the gesture was so quintessentially royal that it should have set Achilles's teeth on edge. But instead he found it so completely her, so entirely Princess Valentina, that it only made him harder. Hotter. More determined to find his way inside her.

And soon.

"I have no objection," he assured her, and there was no pretending his tone wasn't gritty. Harsh. "Are we finished talking?"

And the nerves he'd been unable to detect before were suddenly all over her face. He doubted she knew it. But she was braver than she ought to have been, his deceitful little princess, and all she did was gaze back at him. Clear and sure, as if he couldn't see the soft, vulnerable cast to her mouth.

Or maybe, he thought, she had no idea how transparent she was.

"Yes," Valentina said softly. "I'm ready to stop talking."

And this time, as he drew her to him, he knew it wouldn't end in a kiss. He knew they weren't going to stop until he'd had her at last.

He knew that she was not only going to be his tonight, but she was going to be only his. That no one had ever touched her before, and if he did it right, no one else ever would.

Because Achilles had every intention of ruining his princess for all other men.

CHAPTER SEVEN

VALENTINA COULDN'T BELIEVE this was happening.

At last.

Achilles took her mouth, and there was a lazy quality to his kiss that made her knees feel weak. He set his mouth to hers, and then he took his time. As if he knew that inside she was a jangle of nerves and longing, anticipation and greed. As if he knew she hardly recognized herself or all the needy things that washed around inside her, making her new.

Making her his.

He kissed her for a long while, it seemed to her. He slid his arms around her, he pulled her against his chest, and then he took her mouth with a thoroughness that made a dangerous languor steal all over her. All through her. Until she wasn't sure that she would be able to stand on her own, were he to let go of her.

But he didn't let go.

Valentina thought she might have fallen off the edge of the world anyway, because everything seemed to whirl and cartwheel around, but then she realized that what he'd done was stoop down to bend a little and then pick her up. As if she was as weightless as she felt. He held her in his arms, high against his chest, and she felt her shoes fall off her feet like some kind of punctuation. And when he gazed down into her face, she thought he looked like some kind of conquering warrior of old, though she chided herself for being so fanciful.

There was nothing fanciful about Achilles.

Quite the opposite. He was fierce and masculine and ruthless beyond measure, and still, Valentina couldn't think of anywhere she would rather be—or anyone she would rather be with like this. It all felt inevitable, as if she'd been waiting her whole life for this thing she hardly understood to sweep her away, just like this.

And it had come into focus only when she'd met Achilles.

Because he was her only temptation. She had never wanted anyone else. She couldn't imagine she ever would.

"I don't know what to do," she whispered, aware on some level that he was moving. That he was carrying her up those penthouse stairs as if she weighed nothing at all. But she couldn't bring herself to look away from his dark gold gaze. And the truth was, she didn't care. He could take her anywhere. "I don't want to disappoint you."

"And how would you do that?" His voice was so deep. So lazy and, unless she was mistaken, amused, even as that gaze of his made her quiver, deep inside.

"Well," she stammered out. "Well, I don't—"

"Exactly," he said, interrupting her with that easy

male confidence that she found she liked a little too much. "You don't know, but I do. So perhaps, *glikia mou*, you will allow me to demonstrate the breadth and depth of my knowledge."

And when she shuddered, he only laughed.

Achilles carried her across the top floor, all of which was part of his great master bedroom. It took up the entire top level of his penthouse, bordered on all sides by the wide patio that was also accessible from a separate staircase below. The better to maintain and protect his privacy, she thought now, which she felt personally invested in at the moment. He strode across the hardwood floor with bold-colored rugs tossed here and there, and she took in the exposed brick walls and the bright, modern works of art that hung on them. This floor was all space and silence, and in between there were more of those breathtaking windows that brightened the room with the lights from the city outside.

Achilles didn't turn on any additional light. He simply took Valentina over to the huge bed that was propped up on a sleek modern platform crafted out of a bright, hard steel, and laid her out across it as if she was something precious to him. Which made her heart clutch at her, as if she wanted to be.

And then he stood there beside the bed, his hands on his lean hips, and did nothing but gaze down at her.

Valentina pushed herself up onto her elbows. She could feel her breath moving in and out of her, and it was as if it was wired somehow to all that sensation she could feel lighting her up inside. It made her breasts feel heavier. It made her arms and legs feel somehow restless and sleepy at once.

With every breath, she could feel that bright, hot ache between her legs intensify. And this time, she knew without a shred of doubt that he was aware of every last part of it.

"Do you have anything else to confess?" he asked her, and she wondered if she imagined the dark current in his voice then. But it didn't matter. She had never wanted anyone, but she wanted him. Desperately.

She would confess anything at all if it meant she could have him.

And it wasn't until his eyes blazed, and that remarkable mouth of his kicked up in one corner, that she realized she'd spoken out loud.

"I will keep that in mind," he told her, his voice a rasp into the quiet of the room. Then he inclined his head. "Take off your clothes."

It was as if he'd plugged her into an electrical outlet. She felt zapped. Blistered, perhaps, by the sudden jolt of power. It felt as if there were something bright and hot, wrapped tight around her ribs, pressing down. And down farther.

And she couldn't bring herself to mind.

"But—by myself?" she asked, feeling a little bit light-headed at the very idea. She'd found putting on these jeans a little bit revolutionary. She couldn't imagine stripping them off in front of a man.

And not just any man. Achilles Casilieris.

Who didn't relent at all. "You heard me."

Valentina had to struggle then. She had to somehow

shove her way out of all that wild electrical madness that was jangling through her body, at least enough so she could think through it. A little bit, anyway. She had to struggle to sit up all the way, and then to pull the T-shirt off her body. Her hands went to her jeans next, and she wrestled with the buttons, trying to pull the fly open. It was all made harder by the fact that her hands shook and her fingers felt entirely too thick.

And the more she struggled, the louder her breathing sounded. Until she was sure it was filling up the whole room, and more embarrassing by far, there was no possible way that Achilles couldn't hear it. Or see the flush that she could feel all over her, electric and wild. She wrestled the stiff, unyielding denim down over her hips, that bright heat that churned inside her seeming to bleed out everywhere as she did. She was sure it stained her, marking her bright hot and obvious.

She sneaked a look toward Achilles, and she didn't know what she expected to see. But she froze when her eyes met his.

That dark gold gaze of his was as hot and demanding as ever. That curve in his mouth was even deeper. And there was something in the way that he was looking at her that soothed her. As if his hands were on her already, when they were not. It was as if he was helping her undress when she suspected that it was very deliberate on his part that he was not.

Because of course it was deliberate, she realized in the next breath. He was giving her another choice. He was putting it in her hands, again. And even while part of her found that inordinately frustrating, because she wanted to be swept away by him—or more swept away, anyway—there was still a part of her that relished this. That took pride in the fact that she was choosing to give in to this particular temptation.

That she was choosing to truly offer this particular man the virtue she had always considered such a gift.

It wasn't accidental. She wasn't drunk the way many of her friends had been, nor out of her mind in some other way, or even outside herself in the storm of an explosive temper or wild sensation that had boiled over.

He wanted her to be very clear that she was choosing him.

And Valentina wanted that, too. She wanted to choose Achilles. She wanted this.

She had never wanted anything else, she was sure of it. Not with this fervor that inhabited her body and made her light up from the inside out. Not with this deep certainty.

And so what could it possibly matter that she had never undressed for a man before? She was a princess. She had dressed and undressed in rooms full of attendants her whole life. Achilles was different from her collection of royal aides, clearly. But there was no need for her to be embarrassed, she told herself then. There was no need to go red in the face and start fumbling about, as if she didn't know how to remove a pair of jeans from her own body.

Remember who you are, she chided herself.

She was Princess Valentina of Murin. It didn't matter that seeing her mother might have shaken her. It didn't change a thing. That had nothing to do with who she was, it only meant that she'd become who she was in spite of the choices her mother had made. She could choose to do with that what she liked. And she was choosing to gift her innocence, the virginity she'd clung to as a badge of honor as if that differentiated her from the mother who'd left her, to Achilles Casilieris.

Here. Now.

And there was absolutely nothing to be ashamed about.

Valentina was sure that she saw something like approval in his dark gaze as she finished stripping her jeans from the length of her legs. And then she was sitting there in nothing but her bra and panties. She shifted up and onto her knees. Her hair fell down over her shoulders as she knelt on the bed, swirling across her bared skin and making her entirely too aware of how exposed she was.

But this time it felt sensuous. A sweet, warm sort of reminder of how much she wanted this. Him.

"Go on," he told her, a gruff command.

"That sounded a great deal like an order," Valentina murmured, even as she moved her hands around to her back to work the clasp of her bra. And it wasn't even a struggle to make her voice so airy.

"It was most definitely an order," Achilles agreed, his voice still gruff. "And I would suggest you obey me with significantly more alacrity."

"Or what?" she taunted him gently.

She eased open the silken clasp and then moved her hands around to the bra cups, holding them to her breasts when the bra would have fallen open. "Will you hold it against me in my next performance review? Oh, the horror."

"Are you defying me?"

But Achilles sounded amused, despite his gruffness. And there was something else in his voice then, she thought. A certain tension that she felt move inside her even before she understood what it was. Maybe she didn't have to understand. Her body already knew.

Between her legs, that aching thing grew fiercer. Brighter. And so did she.

"I think you can take it," she whispered.

And then she let the bra fall.

She felt the rush of cooler air over the flesh of her breasts. Her nipples puckered and stung a little as they pulled tight. But what she was concentrating on was that taut, arrested look on Achilles's face. That savage gleam in his dark gold eyes. And the way his fierce, ruthless mouth went flat.

He muttered something in guttural Greek, using words she had never heard before, in her blue-blooded academies and rarefied circles. But she knew, somehow, exactly what he meant.

She could feel it, part of that same ache.

He reached down to grip the hem of his T-shirt, then tugged it up and over his head in a single shrug of one muscled arm. She watched him do it, not certain she was breathing any longer and not able to make herself care about that at all, and then he was moving toward the bed.

Another second and he was upon her.

He swept her up in his arms again, moving her into

the center of the bed, and then he bore her down to the mattress beneath them. And Valentina found that they fit together beautifully. That she knew instinctively what to do.

She widened her legs, he fit himself between them, and she cushioned him there—that long, solid, hard-packed form of his—as if they'd been made to fit together just like this. His bare chest was a wonder. She couldn't seem to keep herself from exploring it, running her palms and her fingers over every ridge and every plane, losing herself in his hot, extraordinary male flesh. She could feel that remarkable ridge of his arousal again, pressed against her right where she ached the most, and it was almost too much.

Or maybe it really was too much, but she wanted it all the same.

She wanted him.

He set his mouth to hers again, and she could taste a kind of desperation on his wickedly clever mouth.

That wild sensation stormed through her, making her limp and wild and desperate for things she'd only ever read about before. He tangled his hands in her hair to hold her mouth to his, then he dropped his chest down against hers, bearing her down into the mattress beneath them. Making her feel glorious and alive and insane with that ache that started between her legs and bloomed out in all directions.

And then he taught her everything.

He tasted her. He moved his mouth from her lips, down the long line of her neck, learning the contours of her clavicle. Then he went lower, sending fire spin-

ning all over her as he made his way down to one of
her breasts, only to send lightning flashing all through
her when he sucked her nipple deep into his mouth.

He tested the weight of her breasts in his faintly
calloused palm, while he played with the nipple of the
other, gently torturing her with his teeth, his tongue,
his cruel lips. When she thought she couldn't take any
more, he switched.

And then he went back and forth, over and over
again, until her head was thrashing against the mattress, and some desperate soul was crying out his name.
Over and over again, as if she might break apart at
any moment.

Valentina knew, distantly, that she was the one making those sounds. But she was too far gone to care.

Achilles moved his way down her body, taking his
sweet time, and Valentina sighed with every inch he
explored. She shifted. She rolled. She found herself
lifting her hips toward him without his having to ask.

"Good girl," he murmured, and it was astonishing
how much pleasure two little words could give her.

He peeled her panties down off her hips, tugged
them down the length of her legs and then threw them
aside. And when he was finished with that, he slid his
hands beneath her bottom as he came back over her,
lifted her hips up into the air and didn't so much as
glance up at her before he set his mouth to the place
where she needed him most.

Maybe she screamed. Maybe she fainted. Maybe
both at once.

Everything seemed to flash bright, then smooth out

into a long, lethal roll of sensation that turned Valentina red hot.

Everywhere.

He licked his way into her. He teased her and he learned her and he tasted her, making even that most private part of her his. She felt herself go molten and wild, and he made a low, rough sound of pleasure, deeply masculine and deliciously savage, and that was too much.

"Oh, no," she heard herself moan. "No—"

Valentina felt more than heard him laugh against the most tender part of her, and then everything went up in flames.

She exploded. She cried out and she shook, the pleasure so intense she didn't understand how anyone could live through it, but still she shook some more. She shook until she thought she'd been made new. She shook until she didn't care either way.

And when she knew her own name again, Achilles was crawling his way over her. He no longer wore those loose black trousers of his, and there was a look of unmistakably savage male triumph stamped deep on his face.

"Beautiful," he murmured. He was on his elbows over her, pressing himself against her. His wall of a chest. That fascinatingly hard part of him below. He studied her flushed face as if he'd never seen her before. "Am I the only man who has ever tasted you?"

Valentina couldn't speak. She could only nod, mute and still shaking.

She wondered if she might shake like this forever,

and she couldn't seem to work herself up into minding if she did.

"Only mine," he said with a certain quiet ferocity that only made that shaking inside her worse. Or better. "You are only and ever mine."

And that was when she felt him. That broad smooth head of his hardest part, nudging against the place where she was nothing but soft, wet heat and longing.

She sucked in a breath, and Achilles took her face in his hands.

"Mine," he said again, in the same intense way.

It sounded a great deal like a vow.

Valentina's head was spinning.

"Yours," she whispered, and he grinned then, too fierce and too elemental.

He shifted his hips and moved a little farther against her, pressing himself against that entrance again, and Valentina found her hands in fists against his chest.

"Will it hurt?" she asked before she knew she meant to speak. "Or is that just something they say in books, to make it seem more..."

But she couldn't quite finish that sentence. And Achilles's gaze was too dark and too bright at once, so intense she couldn't seem to stop shaking or spinning. And she couldn't bring herself to look away.

"It might hurt." He kept his attention on her, fierce and focused. "It might not. But either way, it will be over in a moment."

"Oh." Valentina blinked, and tried to wrap her head around that. "I suppose quick is good."

Achilles let out a bark of laughter, and she wasn't

sure if she was startled or something like delighted to hear it. Both, perhaps.

And it made a knot she hadn't known was hardening inside her chest ease.

"I cannot tell if you are good for me or you will kill me," he told her then. He moved one hand, smoothing her hair back from her temple. "It will only hurt, or feel awkward, for a moment. I promise. As for the rest…"

And the smile he aimed at her then was, Valentina thought, the best thing she'd ever seen. It poured into her and through her, as bright and thick as honey, changing everything. Even the way she shook for him. Even the way she breathed.

"The rest will not be quick," Achilles told her, still braced there above her. "It will not be rushed, it will be thorough. Extremely thorough, as you know I am in all things."

She felt her breath stutter. But he was still going.

"And when I am done, *glikia mou*, we will do it again. And again. Until we get it right. Because I am nothing if not dedicated to my craft. Do you understand me?"

"I understand," Valentina said faintly, because it was hard to keep her voice even when the world was lost somewhere in his commanding gaze. "I guess that's—"

But that was when he thrust his way inside her. It was a quick, hard thrust, slick and hot and overwhelming, until he was lodged deep inside her.

Inside her.

It was too much. It didn't hurt, necessarily, but it

didn't feel good, either. It felt…like everything. Too much of everything.

Too hard. Too long. Too thick and too deep and too—

"Breathe," Achilles ordered her.

But Valentina didn't see how that was possible. How could she breathe when there was a person *inside* her? Even if that person was Achilles.

Especially when that person was Achilles.

Still, she did as he bade her, because he was *inside* her and she was beneath him and splayed open and there was nothing else to do. She breathed in.

She let it out, and then she breathed in again. And then again.

And with each breath, she felt less overwhelmed and more…

Something else.

Achilles didn't seem particularly worried. He held himself over her, one hand tangled in her hair as the other made its way down the front of her body. Lazily. Easily. He played with her breasts. He set his mouth against the crook of her neck where it met her shoulder, teasing her with his tongue and his teeth.

And still she breathed the way he'd told her to do. In. Out.

Over and over, until she couldn't remember that she'd balked at his smooth, intense entry. That she'd ever had a problem at all with *hard* and *thick* and *long* and *deep*.

Until all she could feel was fire.

Experimentally, she moved her hips, trying to get a better feel for how wide he was. How deep. How far inside her own body. Sensation soared through her every time she moved, so she did it again. And again.

She took a little more of him in, then rocked around a little bit, playing. Testing. Seeing how much of him she could take and if it would continue to send licks of fire coursing through her every time she shifted position, no matter how minutely.

It did.

And when she started to shift against him, restlessly, as if she couldn't help herself, Achilles lifted his head and grinned down her, something wild and dark and wholly untamed in his eyes.

It thrilled her.

"Please..." Valentina whispered.

And he knew. He always knew. Exactly what she needed, right when she needed it.

Because that was when he began to move.

He taught her about pace. He taught her depth and rhythm. She'd thought she was playing with fire, but Achilles taught her that she had no idea what real fire was.

And he kept his word.

He was very, very thorough.

When she began to thrash, he dropped down to get closer. He gathered her in his arms, holding her as he thrust inside her, again and again. He made her his with every deep, possessive stroke. He made her want. He made her need.

He made her cry out his name, again and again, until it sounded to Valentina like some kind of song.

This time, when the fire took her, she thought it

might have torn her into far too many pieces for her to ever recover. He lost his rhythm then, hammering into her hard and wild, as if he was as wrecked as she was—

And she held him to her as he tumbled off that edge behind her, and straight on into bliss.

Achilles had made a terrible mistake, and he was not a man who made mistakes. He didn't believe in them. He believed in opportunities—it was how he'd built this life of his. Something that had always made him proud.

But this was a mistake. She was a mistake. He couldn't kid himself. He had never wanted somebody the way that he wanted Valentina. It had made him sloppy. He had concentrated entirely too much on her. Her pleasure. Her innocence, as he relieved her of it.

He hadn't thought to guard himself against her.

He never had to guard himself against anyone. Not since he'd been a child. He'd rather fallen out of the habit—and that notion galled him.

Achilles rolled to the side of the bed and sat there, running a hand over the top of his head. He could hear Valentina behind him, breathing. And he knew what he'd see if he looked. She slept hard, his princess. After he'd finished with her the last time, he'd thought she might have fallen asleep before he'd even pulled out of her. He'd held the weight of her, sprawled there on top of him, her breath heavy and her eyes shut tight so he had no choice but to marvel at the length of her eyelashes.

And it had taken him much longer than it should

have to shift her off him, lay her beside him and cover her with the sheets. Carefully.

It was that unexpected urge to protect her—from himself, he supposed, or perhaps from the uncertain elements of his ruthlessly climate-controlled bedroom— that had made him go cold. Something a little too close to the sort of panic he did not permit himself to feel, ever, had pressed down on him then. And no amount of controlling his breath or ordering himself to stop the madness seemed to help.

He rubbed a palm over his chest now, because his heart was beating much too fast, the damned traitor.

He had wanted her too much, and this was the price. This treacherous place he found himself in now, that he hardly recognized. It hadn't occurred to him to guard himself against a virgin no matter her pedigree, and this was the result.

He felt things.

He felt things—and Achilles Casilieris did not *feel*. He refused to *feel*. The intensity of sex was physical, nothing more. Never more than that, no matter the woman and no matter the situation and no matter how she might beg or plead—

Not that Valentina had done anything of the sort.

He stood from the bed then, because he didn't want to. He wanted to roll back toward her, pull her close again. He bit off a filthy Greek curse, beneath his breath, then moved restlessly across the floor toward the windows.

Manhattan mocked him. It lay there before him, glittering and sparkling madly, and the reason he had a penthouse in this most brash and American of cities was because he liked to stand high above the sprawl of it as if he was some kind of king. Every time he came here he was reminded how far he'd come from his painful childhood. And every time he stayed in this very room, he looked out over all the wealth and opportunity and untethered American dreams that made this city what it was and knew that he had succeeded.

Beyond even the wildest dreams the younger version of Achilles could have conjured up for himself.

But tonight, all he could think about was a copper-haired innocent who had yet to tell him her real name, who had given him all of herself with that sweet enthusiasm that had nearly killed him, and left him… yearning.

And Achilles did not yearn.

He did not yearn and he did not let himself want things he could not have, and he absolutely, positively did not indulge in pointless nostalgia for things he did not miss. But as he stood at his huge windows overlooking Manhattan, the city that seemed to laugh at his predicament tonight instead of welcoming him the way it usually did, he found himself tossed back to the part of his past he only ever used as a weapon.

Against himself.

He hardly remembered his mother. Or perhaps he had beaten that sentimentality out of himself years ago. Either way, he knew that he had been seven or so when she had died, but it wasn't as if her presence earlier had done anything to save her children from the brute of a man whom she had married. Demetrius had been a thick, coarse sort of man, who had worked with his hands down on the docks and had thought that gave him the right to use those hands however he wished. Achilles didn't think there was anything the man had not beaten. His drinking buddies. His wife. The family dog. Achilles and his three young stepsiblings, over and over again. The fact that Achilles had not been Demetrius's own son, but the son of his mother's previous husband who had gone off to war and never returned, had perhaps made the beatings Demetrius doled out harsher—but it wasn't as if he spared his own flesh and blood from his fists.

After Achilles's mother had died under suspicious circumstances no one had ever bothered to investigate in a part of town where nothing good ever happened anyway, things went from bad to worse. Demetrius's temper worsened. He'd taken it out on the little ones, alternately kicking them around and then leaving them for seven-year-old Achilles to raise.

This had always been destined to end in failure, if not outright despair. Achilles understood that now, as an adult looking back. He understood it analytically and theoretically and, if asked, would have said exactly that. He'd been a child himself, etcetera. But where it counted, deep in those terrible feelings he'd turned off when he had still been a boy, Achilles would never understand. He carried the weight of those lives with him, wherever he went. No matter what he built, no matter what he owned, no matter how many times he won this or that corporate battle—none of that paid the ransom he owed on three lives he could never bring back.

They had been his responsibility, and he had failed. That beat in him like a tattoo. It marked him. It was the truth of him.

When it was all over—after Achilles had failed to notice a gas leak and had woken up only when Demetrius had returned from one of his drinking binges three days later to find the little ones dead and Achilles listless and nearly unresponsive himself—everything had changed. That was the cut-and-dried version of events, and it was accurate enough. What it didn't cover was the guilt, the shame that had eaten Achilles alive. Or what it had been like to watch his siblings' tiny bodies carried out by police, or how it had felt to stand at their graves and know that he could have prevented this if he'd been stronger. Bigger. *Better.*

Achilles had been sent to live with a distant aunt who had never bothered to pretend that she planned to give him anything but a roof over his head, and nothing more. In retrospect, that, too, had been a gift. He hadn't had to bother with any healing. He hadn't had to examine what had happened and try to come to terms with it. No one had cared about him or his grief at all.

And so Achilles had waited. He had plotted. He had taken everything that resembled a feeling, shoved it down as deep inside him as it would go, and made it over into hate. It had taken him ten years to get strong enough. To hunt Demetrius down in a sketchy bar in the same bad neighborhood where he'd brutalized Achilles's mother, beaten his own children and left Achilles responsible for what had happened to them.

And that whole long decade, Achilles had told himself that it was an extermination. That he could walk up to this man who had loomed so large over the whole of his childhood and simply rid the world of his unsavory presence. Demetrius did not deserve to live. There was no doubt about that, no shred of uncertainty anywhere in Achilles's soul. Not while Achilles's mother and his stepsiblings were dead.

He'd staked out his stepfather's favorite dive bar, and this one in the sense that it was repellant, not attractive to rich hipsters from affluent neighborhoods. He'd watched a ramshackle, much grayer and more frail version of the stepfather roaring in his head stumble out into the street. And he'd been ready.

He'd gone up to Demetrius out in the dark, cold night, there in a part of the city where no one would ever dream of interfering in a scuffle on the street lest they find themselves shanked. He'd let the rage wash over him, let the sweet taint of revenge ignite in his veins. He'd expected to feel triumph and satisfaction after all these years and all he'd done to make himself strong enough to take this man down—but what he hadn't reckoned with was that the drunken old man wouldn't recognize him.

Demetrius hadn't known who he was.

And that meant that Achilles had been out there in the street, ready to beat down a defenseless old drunk who smelled of watered-down whiskey and a wasted life.

He hadn't done it. It wasn't worth it. He might have happily taken down the violent, abusive behemoth who'd terrorized him at seven, but he'd been too big himself at seventeen to find any honor in felling someone so vastly inferior to him in every way.

Especially since Demetrius hadn't the slightest idea who he'd been.

And Achilles had vowed to himself then and there that the night he stood in the street in his old neighborhood, afraid of nothing save the darkness inside him, would be the absolutely last time he let feelings rule him.

Because he had wasted years. Years that could have been spent far more wisely than planning out the extermination of an old, broken man who didn't deserve to have Achilles as an enemy. He'd walked away from Demetrius and his own squalid past and he'd never gone back.

His philosophy had served him well since. It had led him across the years, always cold and forever calculating his next, best move. Achilles was never swayed by emotion any longer, for good or ill. He never allowed it any power over him whatsoever. It had made him great, he'd often thought. It had made him who he was.

And yet Princess Valentina had somehow reached deep inside him, deep into a place that should have been black and cold and nothing but ice, and lit him on fire all over again.

"Are you brooding?" a soft voice asked from behind him, scratchy with sleep. Or with not enough sleep. "I knew I would do something wrong."

But she didn't sound insecure. Not in the least. She sounded warm, well sated. She sounded like his. She sounded like exactly who she was: the only daughter of one of Europe's last remaining powerhouse kings and the only woman Achilles had ever met who could turn him inside out.

And maybe that was what did it. The suddenly unbearable fact that she was still lying to him. He had this burning thing eating him alive from the inside out, he was cracking apart at the foundations, and she was still lying to him.

She was in his bed, teasing him in that way of hers that no one else would ever dare, and yet she lied to him. Every moment was a lie, even and especially this one. Every single moment she didn't tell him the truth about who she was and what she was doing here was more than a lie. More than a simple deception.

He was beginning to feel it as a betrayal.

"I do not brood," he said, and he could hear the gruffness in his own voice.

He heard her shift on the bed, and then he heard the sound of her feet against his floor. And he should have turned before she reached him, he knew that. He should have faced her and kept her away from him, especially when it was so dark outside and there was still so much left of the night—and he had clearly let it get to him.

But he didn't.

And in a moment she was at his back, and then she was sliding her arms around his waist with a familiarity that suggested she'd done it a thousand times before and knew how perfectly she would fit there. Then she pressed her face against the hollow of his spine.

And for a long moment she simply stood there like

that, and Achilles felt his heart careen and clatter at his ribs. He was surprised that she couldn't hear it—hell, he was surprised that the whole of Manhattan wasn't alerted.

But all she did was stand there with her mouth pressed against his skin, as if she was holding him up, and through him the whole of the world.

Achilles knew that there was any number of ways to deal with this situation immediately. Effectively. No matter what name she called herself. He could call her out. He could ignore it altogether and simply send her away. He could let the darkness in him edge over into cruelty, so she would be the one to walk away.

But the simple truth was that he didn't want to do any of them.

"I have some land," he told her instead, and he couldn't tell if he was appalled at himself or simply surprised. "Out in the West, where there's nothing to see for acres and acres in all directions except the sky."

"That sounds beautiful," she murmured.

And every syllable was an exquisite pain, because he could feel her shape her words. He could feel her mouth as she spoke, right there against the flesh of his back. And he could have understood if it was a sexual thing. If that was what raged in him then. If it took him over and made him want to do nothing more than throw her down and claim her all over again. Sex, he understood. Sex, he could handle.

But it was much worse than that.

Because it didn't feel like fire, it felt…sweet. The kind of sweetness that wrapped around him, crawling into every nook and cranny inside him he'd long ago thought he'd turned to ice. And then stayed there, blooming into something like heat, as if she could melt him that easily.

He was more than a little worried that she could.

That she already had.

"Sometimes a man wants to be able to walk for miles in any direction and see no one," he heard himself say out loud, as if his mouth was no longer connected to the rest of him. "Not even himself."

"Or perhaps especially not himself," she said softly, her mouth against his skin having the same result as before.

Then he could feel her breathe, there behind him. There was a surprising amount of strength in the arms she still wrapped tight around his midsection. Her scent seemed to fill his head, a hint of lavender and something far softer that he knew was hers alone.

And the truth was that he wasn't done. He had never been a casual man in the modern sense, preferring mistresses who understood his needs and could cater to them over longer periods of time to one-night stands and such flashes in the pan that brought him nothing but momentary satisfaction.

He had never been casual, but this… This was nothing but trouble.

He needed to send her away. He had to fire Natalie, make sure that Valentina left, and leave no possible opening for either one of them to ever come back. This needed to be over before it really started. Before he forgot that he was who he was for a very good reason.

Demetrius had been a drunk. He'd cried and apologized when he was sober, however rarely that occurred. But Achilles was the monster. He'd gone to that bar to kill his stepfather, and he'd planned the whole thing out in every detail, coldly and dispassionately. He still didn't regret what he'd intended to do that night—but he knew perfectly well what that made him. And it was not a good man.

And that was all well and good as long as he kept the monster in him on ice, where it belonged. As long as he locked himself away, set apart.

It had never been an issue before.

He needed to get Valentina away from him, before he forgot himself completely.

"Pack your things," he told her shortly.

He shifted so he could look down at her again, drawing her around to his front and taking in the kick of those wide green eyes and that mouth he had sampled again and again and again.

And he couldn't do it.

He wanted her to know him, and even though that was the most treacherous thing of all, once it was in his head he couldn't seem to let it go. He wanted her to know him, and that meant he needed her to trust him enough to tell who she was. And that would never happen if he sent her away right now the way he should have.

And he was so used to thinking of himself as a monster. Some part of him—a large part of him—took a kind of pride in that, if he was honest. He'd worked so hard on making that monster into an impenetrable wall of wealth and judgment, taste and power.

But it turned out that all it took was a deceitful princess to make him into a man.

"I'm taking you to Montana," he told her gruffly, because he couldn't seem to stop himself.

And doomed them both.

CHAPTER EIGHT

ONE WEEK PASSED, and then another, and the six weeks Valentina had agreed to take stretched out into seven, out on Achilles's Montana ranch where the only thing on the horizon was the hint of the nearest mountain range.

His ranch was like a daydream, Valentina thought. Achilles was a rancher only in a distant sense, having hired qualified people to take care of the daily running of the place and turn its profit. Those things took place far away on some or other of his thousands of acres tucked up at the feet of the Rocky Mountains. They stayed in the sprawling ranch house, a sprawling nod toward log cabins and rustic ski lodges, the better to overlook the unspoiled land in all directions.

It was far away from everything and felt even farther than that. It was an hour drive to the nearest town, stout and quintessentially Western, as matter-of-fact as it was practical. They'd come at the height of Montana's short summer, hot during the day and cool at night, with endless blue skies stretching on up toward forever and nothing to do but soak in the quiet. The stunning silence, broken only by the wind. The sun. The exuberant moon and all those improbable, impossible stars, so many they cluttered up the sky and made it feel as if, were she to take a big enough step, Valentina could toss herself straight off the planet and into eternity.

And Valentina knew she was running out of time. Her wedding was the following week, she wasn't who she was pretending she was, and these stolen days in this faraway place of blue and gold were her last with this man. This stolen life had only ever been hers on loan.

But she would have to face that soon enough.

In Montana, as in New York, her days were filled with Achilles. He was too precise and demanding to abandon his businesses entirely, but there was something about the ranch that rendered him less overbearing. He and Valentina would put out what fires there might be in the mornings, but then, barring catastrophe, he let his employees earn their salaries the rest of the day.

While he and Valentina explored what this dreamy ranch life, so far removed from everything, had to offer. He had a huge library that she imagined would be particularly inviting in winter—not, she was forced to remind herself, that she would ever see it in a different season. A guest could sink into one of the deep leather chairs in front of the huge fireplace and read away a snowy evening or two up here in the mountains. He had an indoor pool that let the sky in through its glass ceiling, perfect for swimming in all kinds of weather. There was the hot tub, propped up on its own terrace with a sweeping view, which cried out for those cool evenings. It was a short drive or a long, pretty walk to the lake a little ways up into the mountains, so crisp and clear and cold it almost hurt.

But it was the kind of hurt that made her want more and more, no matter how it made her gasp and think she might lose herself forever in the cut of it.

Achilles was the same. Only worse.

Valentina had always thought of sex—or her virginity, anyway—as a single, solitary thing. Someday she would have sex, she'd always told herself. Someday she would get rid of her virginity. She had never really imagined that it wasn't a single, finite event.

She'd thought virginity, and therefore sex, was the actual breaching of what she still sometimes thought of as her maidenhead, as if she was an eighteenth-century heroine—and nothing more. She'd never really imagined much beyond that.

Achilles taught her otherwise.

Sex with him was threaded into life, a rich undercurrent that became as much a part of it as walking, breathing, eating. It wasn't a specific act. It was everything.

It was the touch of his hand across the dinner table, when he simply threaded their fingers together, the memory of what they'd already done together and the promise of more braided there between them. It was a sudden hot, dark look in the middle of a conversation about something innocuous or work-related, reminding her that she knew him now in so many different dimensions. It was the way his laughter seemed to rearrange her, pouring through her and making her new, every time she heard it.

It was when she stopped counting each new time he wrenched her to pieces as a separate, astonishing event. When she began to accept that he would always do that. Time passed and days rolled on, and all of these things that swirled between them only deepened. He became only more able to wreck her more easily the better he got to know her. And the better she got to know him.

As if their bodies were like the stars above them, infinite and adaptable, a great mess of joy and wonder that time only intensified.

But she knew it was running out.

And the more Achilles called her Natalie—which she thought he did more here, or perhaps she was far more sensitive to it now that she shared his bed—the more her terrible deception seemed to form into a heavy ball in the pit of her stomach, like some kind of cancerous thing that she very much thought might consume her whole.

Some part of her wished it would.

Meanwhile, the real Natalie kept calling her. Again and again, or leaving texts, but Valentina couldn't bring herself to respond to them. What would she say? How could she possibly explain what she'd done?

Much less the fact that she was still doing it and, worse, that she didn't want it to end no matter how quickly her royal wedding was approaching.

Even if she imagined that Natalie was off in Murin doing exactly the same thing with Rodolfo that Valentina was doing here, with all this wild and impossible hunger, what did that matter? They could still switch back, none the wiser. Nothing would change for Valentina. She would go on to marry the prince as she had always been meant to do, and it was highly likely that even Rodolfo himself wouldn't notice the change.

But Natalie had not been sleeping with Achilles before she'd switched places with Valentina. That meant there was no possible way that she could easily step back into the life that Valentina had gone ahead and ruined.

And was still ruining, day by day.

Still, no matter how self-righteously she railed at herself for that, she knew it wasn't what was really bothering her. It wasn't what would happen to Natalie that ate her up inside.

It was what would happen to her. And what could happen with Achilles. She found that she was markedly less sanguine about Achilles failing to notice the difference between Valentina and Natalie when they switched back again. In fact, the very notion made her feel sick.

But how could she tell him the truth? If she couldn't tell Natalie what she'd done, how could she possibly tell the man whom she'd been lying to directly all this time? He thought he was having an affair with his assistant. A woman he had vetted and worked closely with for half a decade.

What was she supposed to say, *Oh, by the way, I'm actually a princess?*

The truth was that she was still a coward. Because she didn't know if what was really holding her back was that she couldn't imagine what she would say—or if she could imagine all too well what Achilles would do. And she knew that made her the worst sort of person. Because when she worried about what he would do, she was worried about herself. Not about how she might hurt him. Not about what it would do to him to learn that she had lied to him all this time. But the fact that it was entirely likely that she would tell him, and that would be the last she'd see of him. Ever.

And Valentina couldn't quite bear for this to be over.

This was her vacation. Her holiday. Her escape— and how had it never occurred to her that if that was true, it meant she had to go back? She'd known that in a general sense, of course, but she hadn't really thought it through. She certainly hadn't thought about what it would feel like to leave Achilles and then walk back to the stifling life she'd called her own for all these years.

It was one thing to be trapped. Particularly when it was all she'd ever known. But it was something else again to see exactly how trapped she was, to leave it behind for a while, and then knowingly walk straight back into that trap, closing the cage door behind her.

Forever.

Sometimes when she lay awake at night listening to Achilles breathe in the great bed next to her, his arms thrown over her as if they were slowly becoming one person, she couldn't imagine how she was ever going to make herself do it.

But time didn't care if she felt trapped. Or torn. It marched on whether she wanted it to or not.

"Are you brooding?" a low male voice asked from

behind her, jolting her out of her unpleasant thoughts. "I thought that was my job, not yours."

Valentina turned from the rail of the balcony that ambled along the side of the master suite, where she was taking in the view and wondering how she could ever fold herself up tight and slot herself back into the life she'd left behind in Murin.

But the view behind her was even better. Achilles lounged against the open sliding glass door, naked save for a towel wrapped around his hips. He had taken her in a fury earlier, pounding into her from behind until she screamed out his name into the pillows, and he'd roared his own pleasure into the crook of her neck. Then he'd left her there on the bed, limp and still humming with all that passion, while he'd gone out for one of his long, brutal runs he always claimed cleared his head.

It had been weeks now, and he still took her breath. Now that she knew every inch of him, she found herself more in awe of him. All that sculpted perfection of his chest, the dark hair that narrowed at his lean hips, dipping down below the towel where she knew the boldest part of him waited.

She'd tasted him there, too. She'd knelt before the fireplace in that gorgeous library, her hands on his thighs as he'd sat back in one of those great leather chairs. He'd played with her hair, sifting strands of it through his fingers as she'd reached into the battered jeans he wore here on the ranch and had pulled him free.

He'd tasted of salt and man, and he'd let her play

with him as she liked. He let her lick him everywhere until she learned his shape. He let her suck him in, then figure out how to make him as wild as he did when he tasted her in this same way. And she'd taken it as a personal triumph when he'd started to grip the chair. And when he'd lost himself inside her mouth, he'd groaned out that name he called her. *Glikia mou.*

Even thinking about it now made that same sweet, hot restlessness move through her all over again.

But time was her enemy. She knew that. And looking at him as he stood there in the doorway and watched her with that dark gold gaze that she could feel in every part of her, still convinced that he could see into parts of her she didn't know how to name, Valentina still didn't know what to do.

If she told him who she was, she would lose what few days with him she had left. This was Achilles Casilieris. He would never forgive her deception. Never. Her other option was never to tell him at all. She would go back to London with him in a few days as planned, slip away the way she'd always intended to do if a week or so later than agreed, and let the real Natalie pick up the pieces.

And that way, she could remember this the way she wanted to do. She could remember loving him, not losing him.

Because that was what she'd done. She understood that in the same way she finally comprehended intimacy. She'd gone and fallen in love with this man who didn't know her real name. This man she could never, ever keep.

Was it so wrong that if she couldn't keep him, she wanted to keep these sun-soaked memories intact?

"You certainly look like you're brooding." There was that lazy note to his voice that never failed to make her blood heat. It was no different now. It was that quick. It was that inevitable. "How can that be? There's nothing here but silence and sunshine. No call to brood about anything. Unless of course, it is your soul that is heavy." And she could have sworn there was something in his gaze then that dared her to come clean. Right then and there. As if, as ever, he knew what she was thinking. "Tell me, Natalie, what is it that haunts you?"

And it was moments like these that haunted her, but she couldn't tell him that. Moments like this, when she was certain that he knew. That he must know. That he was asking her to tell him the truth at last.

That he was calling her the wrong name deliberately, to see if that would goad her into coming clean.

But the mountains were too quiet and there was too much summer in the air. The Montana sky was a blue she'd never seen before, and that was what she felt in her soul. And if there was a heaviness, or a darkness, she had no doubt it would haunt her later.

Valentina wanted to live here. Now. With him. She wanted to *live*.

She had so little time left to truly *live*.

So once again, she didn't tell him. She smiled instead, wide enough to hide the fissures in her heart, and she went to him.

Because there was so little time left that she could do that. So few days left to reach out and touch him the way she did now, sliding her palms against the mouth-watering planes of his chest as if she was memorizing the heat of his skin.

As if she was memorizing everything.

"I don't know what you're talking about," she told him quietly, her attention on his skin beneath her hands. "I never do."

"I am not the mystery here," he replied, and though his voice was still so lazy, so very lazy, she didn't quite believe it. "There are enough mysteries to go around, I think."

"Solve this one, then," she dared him, going up on her toes to press her mouth to his.

Because she might not have truth and she might not have time, but she had this.

For a little while longer, she had this.

Montana was another mistake, because apparently, that was all he did now.

They spent weeks on his ranch, and Achilles made it all worse by the day. Every day he touched her, every day lost himself in her, every day he failed to get her to come clean with him. Every single day was another nail in his coffin.

And then, worse by far to his mind, it was time to leave.

Weeks in Montana, secluded from the rest of the world, and he'd gained nothing but a far deeper and more disastrous appreciation of Valentina's appeal. He hadn't exactly forced her to the light. He hadn't done anything but lose his own footing.

In all those weeks and all that sweet summer sunshine out in the American West, it had never occurred to him that she simply wouldn't tell him. He'd been so sure that he would get to her somehow. That if he had all these feelings churning around inside him, whatever was happening inside her must be far more extreme.

It had never occurred to him that he could lose that bet.

That Princess Valentina had him beat when it came to keeping herself locked up tight, no matter what.

They landed in London in a bleak drizzle that matched his mood precisely.

"You're expected at the bank in an hour," Valentina told him when they reached his Belgravia town house, standing there in his foyer looking as guileless and innocent as she ever had. Even now, when he had tasted every inch of her. Even now, when she was tearing him apart with that serene, untouchable look on her face. "And the board of directors is adamant—"

"I don't care about the bank," he muttered. "Or old men who think they can tell me what to do."

And just like that, he'd had enough.

He couldn't outright demand that Valentina tell him who she really was, because that wouldn't be her telling him of her own volition. It wouldn't be her trusting him.

It's almost as if she knows who you really are, that old familiar voice inside hissed at him. It had been years since he'd heard it, inside him or otherwise. But even though Demetrius had not been able to identify him on the streets when he'd had the chance, Achilles always knew the old man when he spoke. *Maybe she knows exactly what kind of monster you are.*

And a harsh truth slammed into him then, making him feel very nearly unsteady on his feet. He didn't know why it hadn't occurred to him before. Or maybe it had, but he'd shoved it aside out there in all that Montana sky and sunshine. Because he was Achilles Casilieris. He was one of the most sought-after bachelors in all the world. Legions of women chased after him daily, trying anything from trickery to bribery to outright lies about paternity claims to make him notice them. He was at the top of everyone's *most wanted* list.

But to Princess Valentina of Marin, he was nothing but a bit of rough.

She was slumming.

That was why she hadn't bothered to identify herself. She didn't see the point. He might as well have been the pool boy.

And he couldn't take it. He couldn't process it. There was nothing in him but fire and that raw, unquenchable need, and she was so cool. Too cool.

He needed to mess her up. He needed to do something to make all this…wildfire and feeling dissipate before it ate him alive and left nothing behind. Nothing at all.

"What are you doing?" she asked, and he took a little too much satisfaction in that appropriately uncertain note in her voice.

It was only when he saw her move that he realized he was stalking toward her, backing her up out of the gleaming foyer and into one of the town house's elegant sitting rooms. Not that the beauty of a room could do anything but fade next to Valentina.

The world did the same damned thing.

She didn't ask him a silly question like that again. And perhaps she didn't need to. He backed her up to the nearest settee, and took entirely too much pleasure in the pulse that beat out the truth of her need right there in her neck.

"Achilles…" she said hoarsely, but he wanted no more words. No more lies of omission.

No more *slumming*.

"Quiet," he ordered her.

He sank his hands into her gleaming copper hair, then dragged her mouth to his. Then he toppled her down to antique settee and followed her. She was slender and lithe and wild beneath him, rising to meet him with too much need, too much longing.

As if, in the end, this was the only place they were honest with each other.

And Achilles was furious. Furious, or something like it—something close enough that it burned in him as brightly. As lethally. He shoved her skirt up over her hips and she wrapped her legs around his waist, and she was panting already. She was gasping against his mouth. Or maybe he was breathing just as hard.

"Achilles," she said again, and there was something in her gaze then. Something darker than need.

But this was no time for sweetness. Or anything deeper. This was a claiming.

"Later," he told her, and then he took her mouth

with his, tasting the words he was certain, abruptly, he didn't want to hear.

He might be nothing to her but a walk on the wild side she would look back on while she rotted away in some palatial prison, but he would make sure that she remembered him.

He had every intention of leaving his mark.

Achilles tore off his trousers, freeing himself. Then he reached down and found the gusset of her panties, ripping them off and shoving the scraps aside to fit himself to her at last.

And then he stopped thinking about marks and memories, because she was molten hot and wet. She was his. He sank into her, groaning as she encased his length like a hot, tight glove.

It was so good. It was too good.

She always was.

He moved then, and she did, too, that slick, deep slide. And they knew each other so well now. Their bodies were too attuned to each other, too hot and too certain of where this was going, and it was never, ever enough.

He reached between them and pressed his fingers in the place where she needed him most, and felt her explode into a frenzy beneath him. She raised her hips to meet each thrust. She dug her fingers into his shoulders as if she was already shaking apart.

He felt it build in her, and in him, too. Wild and mad, the way it always was.

As if they could tear apart the world this way. As if they already had.

"No one will ever make you feel the way that I do," he told her then, a dark muttering near her ear as she panted and writhed. "No one."

And he didn't know if that was some kind of endearment, or a dire warning.

But it didn't matter, because she was clenching around him then. She gasped out his name, while her body gripped him, then shook.

And he pumped himself into her, wanting nothing more than to roar her damned name. To claim her in every possible way. To show her—

But he did none of that.

And when it was over, when the storm had passed, he pulled himself away from her and climbed to his feet again. And he felt something sharp and heavy move through him as he looked down at her, still lying there half on and half off the antique settee they'd moved a few feet across the floor, because he had done exactly as he set out to do.

He'd messed her up. She looked disheveled and shaky and absolutely, delightfully ravished.

But all he could think was that he still didn't have her. That she was still going to leave him when she was done here. That she'd never had any intention of staying in the first place. It ripped at him. It made him feel something like crazy.

The last time he'd ever felt anything like it, he'd been an angry seventeen-year-old in a foul-smelling street with an old drunk who didn't know who he was. It was a kind of anguish.

It was a grief, and he refused to indulge it. He refused to admit it was ravaging him, even as he pulled his clothes back where they belonged.

And then she made it even worse. She smiled.

She sat up slowly, pushing her skirt back into place and tucking the torn shreds of her panties into one pocket. Then she gazed up at him.

Achilles was caught by that look in her soft green eyes, as surely as if she'd reached out and wrapped her delicate hands around his throat. On some level, he felt as if she had.

"I love you," she said.

They were such small words, he thought through that thing that pounded in him like fear. Like a gong. Such small, silly words that could tear a man down without any warning at all.

And there were too many things he wanted to say then. For example, how could she tell him that she loved him when she wouldn't even tell him her name?

But he shoved that aside.

"That was sex, *glikia mou*," he grated at her. "Love is something different from a whole lot of thrashing around, half-clothed."

He expected her to flinch at that, but he should have known better. This was his princess. If she was cowed at all, she didn't show it.

Instead, she only smiled wider.

"You're the expert on love as in all things, of course," she murmured, because even here, even now, she was the only person alive who had ever dared to tease him. "My mistake."

She was still smiling when she stood up, then walked

around him. As if she didn't notice that he was frozen there in some kind of astonishment. Or as if she was happy enough to leave him to it as she headed toward the foyer and, presumably, the work he'd always adored that seemed to loom over him these days, demanding more time than he wanted to give.

He'd never had a life that interested him more than his empire, until Valentina.

And he didn't have Valentina.

She'd left Achilles standing there with her declaration heavy in his ears. She'd left him half fire and a heart that long ago should have turned to ice. He'd been so certain it had when he was seven and had lost everything, including his sense of himself as anything like good.

He should have known then.

But it wasn't until much later that day—after he'd quizzed his security detail and household staff to discover she'd walked out with nothing but her shoulder bag and disappeared into the gray of the London afternoon—that he'd realized that had been the way his deceitful princess said goodbye.

CHAPTER NINE

VALENTINA COULDN'T KEEP her mind on her duties now that she was back in Murin. She couldn't keep her mind focused at all, come to that. Not on her duties, not on the goings-on of the palace, not on any of the many changes that had occurred since she'd come back home.

She should have been jubilant. Or some facsimile thereof, surely. She had walked back into her well-known, well-worn trap, expecting the same old cage, only to find that the trap wasn't at all what she had imagined it was—and the cage door had been tossed wide open.

When she'd left London that day, her body had still been shivering from Achilles's touch. She hadn't wanted to go. Not with her heart too full and a little bit broken at her own temerity in telling him how she felt when she'd known she had to leave. But it was time for her to go home, and there had been no getting around that. Her wedding to Prince Rodolfo was imminent. As in, the glittering heads of Europe's ancient houses were assembling to cheer on one of their own, and she needed to be there.

The phone calls and texts that she'd been ignoring that whole time, leaving Natalie to deal with it all on her own, had grown frantic. And she couldn't blame her sister, because the wedding was a mere day away. *Your twin sister*, she'd thought, those terms still feeling too unwieldy. She'd made her way to Heathrow Airport and bought herself a ticket on a commercial plane— the first time she'd ever done anything of the sort. One more normal thing to tuck away and remember later.

"Later" meaning after tomorrow, when she would be wed to a man she hardly knew.

It had taken Valentina a bit too long to do the right thing. To do the only possible thing and tear herself away from Achilles the way she should have done a long time ago. She should never have gone with him to Montana. She should certainly never have allowed them to stay there all that time, living out a daydream that could end only one way.

She'd known that going in, and she'd done it anyway. What did that make her, exactly?

Now I am awake, she thought as she boarded the plane. *Now I am awake and that will have to be as good as* alive, *because it's all I have left.*

She hadn't known what to expect from a regular flight into the commercial airport on the island of Murin. Some part of her imagined that she would be recognized. Her face was on the cover of the Murin Air magazines in every seat back, after all. She'd had a bit of a start when she'd sat down in the remarkably uncomfortable seat, pressed up against a snoring matron on one side and a very gray-faced businessman on the other.

But no one had noticed her shocking resemblance to the princess in the picture. No one had really looked at her at all. She flashed Natalie's passport, walked on the plane without any issues and walked off again in Murin without anyone looking at her twice—even though she was quite literally the spitting image of the princess so many were flocking to Murin to see marry her Prince Charming at last.

Once at the palace, she didn't bother trying to sneak in because she knew she'd be discovered instantly—and that would hardly allow Natalie to switch back and escape, would it? So instead she'd walked up to the guard station around the back at the private family entrance, gazed politely at the guard who waited there and waited.

"But the…the princess is within," the guard had stammered. Maybe he was thrown by the fact Valentina was dressed like any other woman her age on the street. Maybe he was taken back because he'd never spoken to her directly before.

Or maybe it was because, if she was standing here in front of him, she wasn't where the royal guard thought she was. Which he'd likely assumed meant she'd sneaked out, undetected.

All things considered, she was happy to let that mystery stand.

Valentina had aimed a conspiratorial smile at the guard. "The princess can't possibly be within, given that I'm standing right here. But it can be our little secret that there was some confusion, if you like."

And then, feeling heavier than she ever had before

and scarred somehow by what she'd gone through with Achilles, she'd walked back in the life she'd left so spontaneously and much too quickly in that London airport.

She'd expected to find Natalie as desperate to leave as she supposed, in retrospect, she had been. Or why else would she have suggested this switch in the first place?

But instead, she'd found a woman very much in love. With Crown Prince Rodolfo of Tissely. The man whom Valentina was supposed to marry the following day.

More than that, Natalie was pregnant.

"I don't know how it happened," Natalie had said, after Valentina had slipped into her bedroom and woken her up—by sitting on the end of the bed and pulling at Natalie's foot until she'd opened her eyes and found her double sitting there.

"Don't you?" Valentina had asked. "I was a virgin, but I had the distinct impression that you had not saved yourself for marriage all these years. Because why would you?"

Natalie had flushed a bit, but then her eyes had narrowed. "*Was* a virgin? Is that the past tense?" She'd blinked. "Not Mr. Casilieris."

But it wasn't the time then for sisterly confessions. Mostly because Valentina hadn't the slightest idea what she could say about Achilles that wasn't…too much. Too much and too unformed and unbearable, somehow, now that it was over. Now that none of it mattered, and never could.

"I don't think that you have a job with him anymore," Valentina had said instead, keeping her voice even. "Because I don't think you want a job with him anymore. You said you were late, didn't you? You're having a prince's baby."

And when Natalie had demurred, claiming that she didn't know one way or the other and it was likely just the stress of inhabiting someone else's life, Valentina had sprung into action.

She'd made it her business to find out, one way or another. She'd assured Natalie that it was simply to put her mind at ease. But the truth was a little more complicated, she admitted to herself as she made her way through the palace.

The fact was, she was relieved. That was what had washed through her when Natalie had confessed not only her love for Rodolfo, but her suspicions that she might be carrying his child. She'd pushed it off as she'd convinced one of her most loyal maids to run out into the city and buy her a few pregnancy tests, just to be certain. She'd shoved it to the side as she'd smuggled the tests back into her rooms, and then had handed them over to Natalie so she could find out for certain.

But there was no denying it. When Natalie had emerged from the bathroom with a dazed look on her face and a positive test in one hand, Valentina finally admitted the sheer relief that coursed through her veins. It was like champagne. Fizzy and a little bit sharp, washing through her and making her feel almost silly in response.

Because if Natalie was having Rodolfo's baby, there was no possible way that Valentina could marry him.

The choice—though it had always been more of an expected duty than a choice—was taken out of her hands.

"You will marry him," Valentina had said quietly. "It is what must happen."

Natalie had looked pale. "But you… And I'm not… And you don't understand, he…"

"All of that will work out," Valentina had said with a deep certainty she very badly wanted to feel. Because it had to work out. "The important thing is that you will marry him in the morning. You will have his baby and you will be his queen when he ascends the throne. Everything else is spin and scandal, and none of that matters. Not really."

And so it was.

Once King Geoffrey had been brought into the loop and had been faced with the irrefutable evidence that his daughter had been stolen from him all those years ago—that Erica had taken Natalie and, not only that, had told Geoffrey that Valentina's twin had died at birth—he was more than on board with switching the brides at the wedding.

He'd announced to the gathered crowd that a most blessed miracle had occurred some months before. A daughter long thought dead had returned to him to take her rightful place in the kingdom, and they'd all kept it a secret to preserve everyone's privacy as they'd gotten to know each other.

Including Rodolfo, who had always been meant to be part of the family, the king had reminded the assembled crowd and the whole of the world, no matter how. And feelings had developed between Natalie and Rodolfo, where there had only ever been duty and honor between Valentina and her intended.

Valentina had seen this and stepped aside of her own volition, King Geoffrey had told the world. There had been no scandal, no sneaking around, no betrayals. Only one sister looking out for another.

The crowds ate it up. The world followed suit. It was just scandalous enough to be both believable and newsworthy. Valentina was branded as something of a Miss Lonely Hearts, it was true, but that was neither here nor there. The idea that she would sacrifice her fairy-tale wedding—and her very own Prince Charming—for her long-lost sister captured the public's imagination. She was more popular than ever, especially at home in Murin.

And this was a good thing, because now that her father had two heirs, he could marry one of his daughters off to fulfill his promises to the kingdom of Tissely, and he could prepare the other to take over Murin and keep its throne in the family.

And just like that, Valentina went from a lifetime preparing to be a princess who would marry well and support the king of a different country, to a new world in which she was meant to rule as queen in her own right.

If it was another trap, another cage, it was a far more spacious and comfortable one than any she had known before.

She knew that. There was no reason at all she should have been so unhappy.

"Your attention continues to drift, daughter," King Geoffrey said then.

Valentina snapped herself out of those thoughts in her head that did her no good and into the car where she sat with her father, en route to some or other glittering gala down at the water palace on the harbor. She couldn't even remember which charity it was this week. There was always another.

The motorcade wound down from the castle, winding its way along the hills of the beautiful capital city toward the gleaming Mediterranean Sea. Valentina normally enjoyed the view. It was pretty, first and foremost. It was home. It reminded her of so many things, of her honor and her duty and her love of her country. It renewed her commitment to her kingdom, and made her think about all the good she hoped she could do as its sovereign.

And yet these days, she wasn't thinking about Murin. All she could seem to think about was Achilles.

"I am preparing myself for the evening ahead," Valentina replied calmly enough. She aimed a perfectly composed smile at her father. "I live in fear of greeting a diplomat with the wrong name and causing an international incident."

Her father's gaze warmed, something that happened more often lately than it ever had before. Valentina chalked that up to the rediscovery of Natalie and, with it, some sense of family that had been missing before. Or too caught up in the past, perhaps.

"I have never seen you forget a name in all your life," Geoffrey said. "It's one among many reasons I expect you will make a far better queen than I have been a king. And I am aware I gave you no other choice, but

I cannot regret that your education and talents will be Murin's gain, not Tissely's."

"I will confess," Valentina said then, "that stepping aside so that Natalie could marry Rodolfo is not quite the sacrifice some have made it out to be."

Her father's gaze then was so canny that it reminded her that whatever else he was, King Geoffrey of Marin was a force to be reckoned with.

"I suspected not," he said quietly. "But there is no reason not to let them think so. It only makes you more sympathetic."

His attention was caught by something on his phone then. And as he frowned down at it, Valentina looked away. Back out the window to watch the sun drip down over the red-tipped rooftops that sloped all the way to the crystal blue waters below.

She let her hand move, slowly so that her father wouldn't notice, and held it over that faint roundness low in her belly she'd started to notice only a few weeks ago.

If her father thought she was a sympathetic figure now, she thought darkly, he would be delighted when she announced to him and the rest of the world that she was going to be a mother.

A single mother. A princess destined for his throne, with child.

Her thoughts went around and around, keeping her up at night and distracting her by day. And there were never any answers or, rather, there were never any good answers. There were never any answers she liked. Shame and scandal were sure to follow anything she did, or didn't do for that matter. There was no possible way out.

And even if she somehow summoned the courage to tell her father, then tell the kingdom, and then, far more intimidating, tell Achilles—what did she think might happen then? As a princess with no path to the throne, she had been expected to marry the Crown Prince of Tissely. As the queen of Murin, by contrast, she would be expected to marry someone of equally impeccable lineage. There were only so many such men alive, Valentina had met all of them, and none of them were Achilles.

No one was Achilles. And that shouldn't have mattered to her. There were so many other things she needed to worry about, like this baby she was going to be able to hide for only so long.

But he was the only thing she could seem to think about, even so.

The gala was as expected. These things never varied much, which was both their charm and their curse. There was an endless receiving line. There were music and speeches, and extremely well-dressed people milling about complimenting each other on the same old things. A self-congratulatory trill of laughter here, a fake smile there, and so it went. Dignitaries and socialites rubbing shoulders and making money for this or that cause the way they always did.

Valentina danced with her father, as tradition dictated. She was pleased to see Rodolfo and Natalie, freshly back from their honeymoon and exuding exactly the sort of happy charm that made everyone root for them, Valentina included.

Valentina especially, she thought.

She excused herself from the crush as soon as she could, making her way out onto one of the great balconies in this water palace that took its cues from far-off Venice and overlooked the sea. Valentina stood there for a long while, helplessly reliving all the things she'd been so sure she could lock away once she came back home. Over and over—

And she thought that her memory had gotten particularly sharp—and cruel. Because when she heard a foot against the stones behind her and turned, her smile already in place the way it always was, she saw him.

But it couldn't be him, of course. She assumed it was her hormones mixing with her memory and making her conjure him up out of the night air.

"Princess Valentina," Achilles said, and his voice was low, a banked fury simmering there in every syllable. "I do not believe we have been introduced properly. You are apparently of royal blood you sought to conceal and I am the man you thought you could fool. How pleasant to finally make your acquaintance."

It occurred to her that she wasn't fantasizing at the same moment it really hit her that he was standing before her. Her heart punched at her. Her stomach sank.

And in the place she was molten for him, instantly, she ached. Oh, how she ached.

"Achilles…"

But her throat was so dry. It was in marked contrast to all that emotion that flooded her eyes at the sight of him that she couldn't seem to control.

"Are those tears, Princess?" And he laughed then. It was a dark, angry sort of sound. It was not the kind of laughter that made the world shimmer and change. And still, it was the best sound Valentina had heard in weeks. "Surely those are not tears. I cannot think of a single thing you have to cry about, Valentina. Not one. Whereas I have a number of complaints."

"Complaints?"

All she could seem to do was echo him. That and gaze at him as if she was hungry, and the truth was that she was. She couldn't believe he was here. She didn't care that he was scowling at her—her heart was kicking at her, and she thought she'd never seen anything more beautiful than Achilles Casilieris in a temper, right here in Murin.

"We can start with the fact that you lied to me about who you are," he told her. "There are numerous things to cover after that, culminating in your extremely bad decision to walk out. *Walk out*." He repeated it with three times the fury. "On *me*."

"Achilles." She swallowed, hard. "I don't think—"

"Let me be clear," he bit out, his dark gold gaze blazing as he interrupted her. "I am not here to beg or plead. I am Achilles Casilieris, a fact you seem to have forgotten. I do not beg. I do not plead. But I feel certain, princess, that you will do both."

He had waited weeks.

Weeks.

Having never been walked out on before—ever—Achilles had first assumed that she would return. Were not virgins forever making emotional connections with the men who divested them of their innocence? That was the reason men of great experience generally avoided virgins whenever possible. Or so he thought, at any rate. The truth was that he could hardly remember anything before Valentina.

Still, he waited. When the royal wedding happened the day after she'd left, and King Geoffrey made his announcement about his lost daughter—who, he'd realized, was his actual assistant and also, it turned out, a royal princess—Achilles had been certain it was only a matter of time before Valentina returned to London.

But she never came.

And he did not know when it had dawned on him that this was something he was going to have to do himself. The very idea enraged him, of course. That she had walked out on him at all was unthinkable. But what he couldn't seem to get his head around was the fact that she didn't seem to have seen the error of her ways, no matter how much time he gave her to open her damned eyes.

She was too beautiful and it was worse now, he thought darkly, here in her kingdom, where she was no longer pretending anything.

Tonight she was dressed like the queen she would become one day, all of that copper hair piled high on the top of her head, jewels flashing here and there. Instead of the pencil skirts he'd grown accustomed to, she wore a deep blue gown that clung to her body in a way that was both decorous and alluring at once. And if he was not mistaken, made her curves seem more voluptuous than he recalled.

She was much too beautiful for Achilles's peace of mind, and worse, she did not break down and begin the begging or the pleading, as he would have preferred. He could see that her eyes were damp, though the tears that had threatened seemed to have receded. She smoothed her hand over her belly, as if the dress had wrinkles when it was very clear that it did not, and when she looked up from that wholly unnecessary task her green eyes were as guarded as her smile was serene.

As if he was a stranger. As if he had never been so deep inside her she'd told him she couldn't breathe.

"What are you doing here?" she asked.

"That is the wrong question."

She didn't so much as blink, and that smile only deepened. "I had no idea that obscure European charities were of such interest to men of your stature, and I am certain it was not on your schedule."

"Are you questioning how I managed to score an invite?" he asked, making no particular move to keep the arrogant astonishment from his voice. "Perhaps I must introduce myself again. There is no guest list that is not improved by my presence, princess. Even yours."

Her gaze became no less guarded. Her expression did not change. But still, Achilles thought something in her steeled. And her shoulders straightened almost imperceptibly.

"I must apologize to you," she said, very distinctly.

And this was what Achilles had wanted. It was why

he'd come here. He had imagined it playing out almost exactly this way.

Except there was something in her tone that rubbed him the wrong way, now that it was happening. It was that guarded look in her eyes perhaps. It was the fact that she didn't close the distance between them, but stayed where she was, one hand on the balcony railing and the other at her side. As distant as if she was on some magazine cover somewhere instead of standing there in front of him.

He didn't like this at all.

"You will have to be more specific, I am afraid," he said coolly. "I can think of a great many apologies you owe me."

Her mouth curved, though he would not call it a smile, precisely.

"I walked into a bathroom in an airport in London and saw a woman I had never met before, who could only be my twin. I could not resist switching places with her." Valentina glanced toward the open doors and the gala inside, as if it called to her more than he did, and Achilles hated that, too. Then she looked back at him, and her gaze seemed darker. "Do not mistake me. This is a good life. It is just that it's a very specific, very planned sort of life and it involves a great many spotlights. I wanted a normal one, for a change. Just for a little while. It never occurred to me that that decision could affect anyone but me. I would never have done it if I ever thought that you—"

But Achilles couldn't hear this. Because it sounded entirely too much like a postmortem. When he had traveled across Europe to find her because he couldn't bear the thought that it had already ended, or that he hadn't picked up on the fact that she was leaving him until she'd already gone.

"Do you need me to tell you that I love you, Valentina?" he demanded, his voice low and furious. "Is that what this is? Tell me what you need to hear. Tell me what it will take."

She jolted as if he'd slapped her. And he hated that, so he took the single step that closed the distance between them, and then there was no holding himself back. Not when she was so close again—at last—after all these weeks. He reached over and wrapped his hands around her shoulders, holding her there at arm's length, like some kind of test of his self-control. He thought that showed great restraint, when all he wanted was to haul her toward him and get his mouth on her.

"I don't need anything," she threw at him in a harsh sort of whisper. "And I'm sorry you had to find out who I was after I left. I couldn't figure out how to tell you while I was still with you. I didn't want to ruin—"

She shook her head, as if distressed.

Achilles laughed. "I knew from almost the first moment you stepped on the plane in London. Did you imagine I would truly believe you were Natalie for long? When you could not perform the most basic of tasks she did daily? I knew who you were within moments after the plane reached its cruising altitude."

Her green eyes went wide with shock. Her lips parted. Even her face paled.

"You knew?"

"You have never fooled me," he told her, his voice getting a little too low. A little too hot. "Except perhaps when you claimed you loved me, then left."

Her eyes overflowed then, sending tears spilling down her perfect, elegant cheeks. And he was such a bastard that some part of him rejoiced.

Because if she cried for him, she wasn't indifferent to him. She was certainly not immune to him.

It meant that it was possible he hadn't ruined this, after all, the way he did everything else. It meant it was possible this was salvageable.

He didn't like to think about what it might mean if it wasn't.

"Achilles," she said again, more distinctly this time. "I never saw you coming—it never occurred to me that I could ever be anything but honorable, because I had never been tempted by anything in my life. Only you. The only thing I lied to you about was my name. Everything else was true. Is true." She shook her head. "But it's hopeless."

"Nothing is hopeless," he growled at her. "I have no intention of losing you. I don't lose."

"I'm not talking about a loss," she whispered fiercely, and he could feel a tremor go through her. "This isn't a game. You are a man who is used to doing everything in his own way. You are not made for protocol and diplomacy and the tedious necessities of excruciating propriety. That's not who you are." Her chin tilted up slightly. "But I'm afraid it is exactly who I am."

"I'm not a good man, *glikia mou*," he told her then,

not certain what was gripping him. He only knew he couldn't let her go. "But you know this. I have always known who I am. A monster in fine clothes, rubbing shoulders with the elites who would spit on me if they could. If they did not need my money and my power."

Achilles expected a reaction. He expected her to see him at last as she had failed to see him before. The scales would fall from her eyes, perhaps. She would recoil, certainly. He had always known that it would take so very little for people to see the truth about him, lurking right there beneath his skin. Not hidden away at all.

But Valentina did not seem to realize what had happened. She continued to look at him the way she always did. There wasn't the faintest flicker of anything like revulsion, or bleak recognition, in her gaze.

If anything, her gaze seemed warmer than before, for all it was wet. And that made him all the more determined to show her what she seemed too blind to see.

"You are not hearing me, Valentina. I'm not speaking in metaphors. Do you have any idea what I have done? The lives that I have ruined?"

She smiled at that, through her tears. "I know exactly who you are," she said, with a bedrock certainty that shook him. "I worked for you. You did not wine me or dine me. You did not take me on a fancy date or try to impress me in any way. You treated me like an assistant, an underling, and believe me, there is nothing more revealing. Are you impatient? Are you demanding and often harsh? Of course." She shrugged, as if this was all so obvious it was hardly worth talking about. "You are a very powerful man. But you are not a monster."

If she'd reached over and wrenched his mangled little heart from between his ribs with her elegant hands and then held it there in front of him, it could not possibly have floored him more.

"And you will not convince me otherwise," she added, as if she could see that he was about to say something. "There's something I have to tell you. And it's entirely possible that you are not going to like it at all."

Achilles blinked. "How ominous."

She blew out a breath. "You must understand that there are no good solutions. I've had no idea how to tell you this, but our… What happened between us had consequences."

"Do you think that I don't know that?" he belted out at her, and he didn't care who heard him. He didn't care if the whole of her pretty little kingdom poured out of the party behind them to watch and listen. "Do you think that I would be here if I was unaware of the consequences?"

"I'm not talking about feelings—"

"I am," he snapped. "I have not felt anything in years. I have not wanted to feel. And thanks to you all I do now is feel. Too damned much, Valentina." She hadn't actually ripped his heart out, he reminded himself. It only felt as if she had. He forced himself to loosen his grip on her before he hurt her. "And it doesn't go anywhere. Weeks pass, and if anything grows worse."

"Achilles, please," she whispered, and the tears were falling freely again. "I never wanted to hurt you."

"I wish you had hurt me," he told her, something

dark and bitter, and yet neither of those things threaded through him. "Hurt things heal. This is far worse."

She sucked in a breath as if he'd punched her. He forged on, throwing all the doom and tumult inside him down between them.

"I have never loved anything in my life, Princess. I have wanted things and I've taken them, but love has always been for other men. Men who are not monsters by any definition. Men who have never ruined anything—not lives, not companies and certainly not perfect, virginal princesses who had no idea what they were signing up for." He shook his head. "But there is nothing either one of us can do about it now. I'm afraid the worst has already happened."

"The worst?" she echoed. "Then you know...?"

"I love you, *glikia mou*," he told her. "There can be no other explanation, and I feel sorry for you, I really do. Because I don't think there's any going back."

"Achilles..." she whispered, and that was not a look of transported joy on her face. It wasn't close. "I'm so sorry. Everything is different now. I'm pregnant."

CHAPTER TEN

ACHILLES WENT SILENT. Stunned, if Valentina had to guess.

If that frozen astonishment in his dark gold gaze was any guide.

"And I am to be queen," she told him, pointedly. His hands were still clenched on her shoulders, and what was wrong with her that she should love that so much? That she should love any touch of his. That it should make her feel so warm and safe and wild with desire. All at once. "My father thought that he would not have an heir of his own blood, because he thought he had only one daughter. But now he has two, and Natalie has married Rodolfo. That leaves me to take the throne."

"I'm not following you," Achilles said, his voice stark. Something like frozen. "I can think of no reason that you have told me in one breath that I am to be a father and in the next you feel you must fill me in on archaic lines of succession."

"There is very strict protocol," she told him, and her voice cracked. She slid her hands over her belly. "My father will never accept—"

"You keep forgetting who I am," Achilles growled, and she didn't know if he'd heard a word she'd said. "If you are having my child, Valentina, this conversation is over. We will be married. That's an end to it."

"It's not that simple."

"On the contrary, there is nothing simpler."

She needed him to understand. This could never be. They could never happen. She was trapped just as surely as she'd ever been. Why couldn't he see that? "I am no longer just a princess. I'm the Crown Princess of Murin—"

"Princess, princess." Achilles shook his head. "Tell me something. Did you mean it when you told me that you loved me? Or did you only dare to tell me in the first place because you knew you were leaving?"

That walloped Valentina. She thought that if he hadn't been holding on to her, she would have staggered and her knees might well have given out from beneath her.

"Don't be ridiculous." But her voice was barely a whisper.

"Here's the difference between you and me, princess. I have no idea what love is. All I know is that you came into my life and you altered something in me." He let go of her shoulder and moved his hand to cover his heart, and broke hers that easily. "Here. It's changed now, and I can't change it back. And I didn't tell you these things and then leave. I accepted these things, and then came to find you."

She felt blinded. Panicked. As if all she could do

was cower inside her cage—and worse, as if that was what she wanted.

"You have no idea what you're talking about," she told him instead. "You might be a successful businessman, but you know nothing about the realities of a kingdom like Murin."

"I know you better than you think. I know how desperate you are for a normal life. Isn't that why you switched places with Natalie?" His dark gaze was almost kind. "But don't you understand? Normal is the one thing you can never be, *glikia mou*."

"You have no idea what you're talking about," she said again, and this time her voice was even softer. Fainter.

"You will never be normal, Valentina," Achilles said quietly. His fingers tightened on her shoulder. "I am not so normal myself. But together, you and I? We will be extraordinary."

"You don't know how much I wish that could happen." She didn't bother to wipe at her tears. She let them fall. "This is a cage, Achilles. I'm trapped in it, but you're not. And you shouldn't be."

He let out a breath that was too much like a sigh, and Valentina felt it shudder through her, too. Like foreboding.

"You can live in fear, or you can live the life you want, Valentina," he told her. "You cannot do both."

His dark gaze bored into her, and then he dropped his other hand, so he was no longer touching her.

And then he made it worse and stepped back.

She felt her hands move, when she hadn't meant to

move at all. Reaching out for him, whether she wanted to or not.

"If you don't want to be trapped, don't be trapped," Achilles said, as if it was simple. And with that edge in his voice that made her feel something a little more pointed than simply restless. "I don't know how to love, but I will learn. I have no idea how to be a father, but I will dedicate myself to being a good one. I never thought that I'd be a husband to anyone, but I will be the husband you need. You can sit on your throne. You can rule your kingdom as you wish. I have no need to be a king. But I will be one for you." He held out his hand. "All you have to do is be brave, princess. That's all. Just be a little brave."

"It's a cage, Achilles," she told him again, her voice ragged. "It's a beautiful, beautiful cage, this life. And there's no changing it. It's been the same for untold centuries."

"Love me," he said then, like a bomb to her heart. What was left of it. "I dare you."

And the music poured out from the party within. Inside, her father ruled the way he always did, and her brand-new sister danced with the man Valentina had always imagined she would marry. Natalie had come out of nowhere and taken her rightful place in the kingdom, and the world hadn't ended when brides had been switched at a royal wedding. If anything, life had vastly improved for everyone involved. Why wasn't that the message Valentina was concentrating on?

She realized that all this time, she'd been focused on what she couldn't do. Or what she had to do. She'd been consumed with duty, honor—but none of it her choice. All of it thrust upon her by an accident of birth. If Erica had taken Valentina instead of Natalie, she would have met Achilles some time ago. They wouldn't be standing here, on this graceful balcony, overlooking the soothing Mediterranean and her father's kingdom.

Her whole life seemed to tumble around before her, year after year cracking open before her like so many fragile eggs against the stones beneath her feet. All the things she never questioned. All the certainties she simply accepted, because what was the alternative? She'd prided herself on her serenity in the face of anything that had come her way. On her ability to do what was asked of her, always. What was expected of her, no matter how unfair.

And she'd never really asked herself what she wanted to do with her life. Because it had never been a factor. Her life had been meticulously planned from the start.

But now Achilles stood before her, and she carried their baby inside her. And she knew that as much as she wanted to deny it, what he said was true. She was a coward. She'd used her duty to hide behind. She could have stayed in London, could have called off her wedding. But she hadn't.

And had she really imagined she could walk down that aisle to Rodolfo, having just left Achilles in London? Had she really intended to do that?

It was unimaginable. And yet she knew she'd meant to do exactly that.

She'd been saved from that vast mistake, and yet here she was, standing in front of the man she loved, coming up with new reasons why she couldn't have the one thing in her life she ever truly wanted.

All this time she'd been convinced that her life was the cage. That her royal blood trapped her.

But the truth was, she was the one who did that.

She was her own cage, and she always would be if she didn't do something to stop it right now. If she didn't throw open the door, step through the opening and allow herself to reach out for the man she already knew she loved.

Be brave, he'd told her, as if he knew she could do it. As if he had no doubt at all.

"I love you," she whispered helplessly. Lost somewhere in that gaze of his, and the simple fact that he was here. Right here in front of her, his hand stretched toward her, waiting for her with a patience she would have said Achilles Casilieris did not possess.

"Marry me, *glikia mou*. And you can love me forever." His mouth crept up in one corner, and all the scars Valentina had dug into her own heart when she'd left him seemed to glow a little bit. Then knit themselves into something more like art. "I'm told that's how it goes. But you know me. I always like to push the boundaries a little bit farther."

"Farther than forever?"

And she smiled at him then, not caring if she was still crying. Or laughing. Or whatever was happening inside her that was starting to take her over.

Maybe that was what it was to be brave. Doing whatever it was not because she felt it was right, but because it didn't matter what she felt. It was right, so she had to do it.

"Three forevers," Achilles said, as if he was promising them to her, here and now. "To start."

And he was still holding out his hand.

"Breathe," he murmured, as if he could see all the tumult inside her.

Valentina took a deep breath. She remembered lying in that bed of his with all of New York gleaming around them. He'd told her to breathe then, too.

In. Out.

Until she felt a little less full, or a little more able to handle what was happening. Until she had stopped feeling overwhelmed, and had started feeling desperate with need.

And this was no different.

Valentina breathed in, then out. Then she stepped forward and slid her hand into his, as easily as if they'd been made to fit together just like that, then let him pull her close.

He shifted to take her face in his hands, tilting her head back so he could fit his mouth to hers. Though he didn't. Not yet.

"Forever starts now," Valentina whispered. "The first one, anyway."

"Indeed." Achilles's mouth was so deliriously hard, and directly over hers. "Kiss me, Valentina. It's been too long."

And Valentina did more than kiss him. She poured herself into him, pushing herself up on her toes and winding her arms around his neck, and that was just the start.

Because there was forever after forever stacked up in front of them, just waiting for them to fill it. One after the next.

Together.

CHAPTER ELEVEN

ACHILLES MADE A terrible royal consort.

He didn't know who took more pride in that, he himself or the press corps, who finally had the kind of access to him they'd always wanted, and adored it.

But he didn't much care how bad he was at being the crown princess's billionaire, as long as he had Valentina. She allowed him to be as surly as he pleased, because she somehow found that charming. She'd even supported him when he'd refused to allow her father to give him a title, because he had no wish to become a Murinese citizen.

"I thank you," he had said to Geoffrey. "But I prefer not to swear my fealty to my wife by law, and title. I prefer to do it by choice."

Their wedding had been another pageant, with all the pomp and circumstance anyone could want for Europe's favorite princess. Achilles had long since accepted the fact that the world felt it had a piece of their story. Or of Valentina, certainly.

And he was a jealous bastard, but he tried not to mind as she waved and smiled and gave them what they wanted.

Meanwhile, as she grew bigger with his child she seemed to glow more by the day, and all those dark things in him seemed to grow lighter every time she smiled at him.

So he figured it was a draw.

She told him he wasn't a monster with that same deep certainty, as if she'd been there. As if she knew. And every time she did, he was more and more tempted to believe her.

She gave birth to their son the following spring, right about the time her sister was presenting the kingdom of Tissely with a brand-new princess of their own, because the ways in which the twins were identical became more and more fascinating all the time. The world loved that, too.

But not as much as Valentina and Natalie did.

And as Achilles held the tiny little miracle that he and Valentina had made, he felt another lock fall into place inside him. Maybe they could not be normal, Valentina and him. But that only meant that the love they would lavish on this child would be no less than remarkable.

And no less than he deserved.

This child would never live in the squalor his father had. He would never want for anything. No hand would be raised against him, and no fists would ever make contact with his perfect, sweet face. His parents would not abandon him, no stepfathers would abuse him, and it was entirely possible that he would be so loved that the world might drown in the force of it. Achilles would not be at all surprised.

Achilles met his beautiful wife's gaze over their

child's head, lying with her in the bed in their private wing of the hospital. The public was locked outside, waiting to meet this latest member of the royal family. But that would happen later.

Here, now, it was only the three of them. His brand-new family and the world he would build for him. The world that Valentina would give their son.

Just as she'd given it to him.

"You are mine, *glikia mou*," he said softly as her gaze met his. Fiercely. "More now than ever."

And he knew that Valentina remembered. The first vows they'd taken, though neither of them had called it that, in his New York penthouse so long ago.

The smile she gave him then was brighter than the sun, and warmed him all the same. Their son wriggled in his arms, as if he felt it, too. His mother's brightness that had lit up a monster lost in his own darkness, and convinced him he was a man.

Not just a man, but a good one. For her.

Anything for her.

"Yours," she agreed softly.

And Achilles reckoned that three forevers would not be nearly enough with Valentina.

But he was Achilles Casilieris. Perfection was his passion.

If they needed more forever they'd have it, one way or another.

He had absolutely no doubt.

* * * * *

If you enjoyed
THE BILLIONAIRE'S SECRET PRINCESS
don't forget to read the first part of Caitlin Crews's
SCANDALOUS ROYAL BRIDES duet,

THE PRINCE'S NINE-MONTH SCANDAL

Available now!

Available July 18, 2017

#3545 AN HEIR MADE IN THE MARRIAGE BED
by Anne Mather

When Joanna requests a divorce from Matt Novak, he makes one thing clear: he expects them to remain *intimately* married! Tempers flare, and they give in to the thrill of each other's touch—but then Joanna discovers she's carrying Matt's baby!

#3546 THE PRINCE'S STOLEN VIRGIN
Once Upon a Seduction...
by Maisey Yates

Briar Harcourt cannot believe she is a long-lost princess. But now Prince Felipe has found Briar—and she's his intended bride! Felipe's desire for her is unexpected, but searing...and he'll seduce her into surrender...

#3547 PROTECTING HIS DEFIANT INNOCENT
Bound to a Billionaire
by Michelle Smart

Continuing her brother's charitable work, Francesca Pellegrini finds herself under Felipe Lorenzi's protection. His commands infuriate her, but every look invites her to abandon her innocence...especially when lone wolf Felipe decides to make her his!

#3548 PREGNANT AT ACOSTA'S DEMAND
by Maya Blake

Ramon Acosta once gave Suki unimaginable pleasure. Her unexpected pregnancy ended tragically—but now Ramon is determined that Suki will provide his heir! His outrageous demand reignites both Suki's longing for a child *and* the burning memory of his touch...

HPCNM0717RA

#3549 CARRYING THE SPANIARD'S CHILD
Secret Heirs of Billionaires
by Jennie Lucas
After one night with ruthless Santiago Velazquez, Belle Langtry finds herself carrying a miraculous baby! Belle's news shocks Santiago—he won't let her escape his claim to her *and* their child! His plan? To bind Belle with his ring!

#3550 THE SECRET HE MUST CLAIM
The Saunderson Legacy
by Chantelle Shaw
Elin Saunderson's night with mysterious Cortez left her pregnant! A year later she learns that he will inherit her adopted father's fortune. Cortez Ramos sees one tempting solution: a marriage of convenience, legitimizing his heir *and* returning Elin to his bed!

#3551 A RING FOR THE GREEK'S BABY
One Night With Consequences
by Melanie Milburne
Loukas Kyprianos's wild night with innocent Emily Seymour was unforgettable. But then he finds out that Emily is carrying his child! Emily doesn't expect a fairy tale—but when the Greek's protection turns to seduction, how long will it be before she succumbs?

#3552 BOUGHT FOR THE BILLIONAIRE'S REVENGE
by Clare Connelly
Being forced to spurn Nikos Kyriazis devastated Marnie Kenington. Years later, he offers to absolve her family's bankruptcy—*if* she marries him! Nikos wants revenge—and he knows that in the bedroom he can take Marnie apart, piece by sensual piece...

YOU CAN FIND MORE INFORMATION ON UPCOMING HARLEQUIN® TITLES, FREE EXCERPTS AND MORE AT WWW.HARLEQUIN.COM.

HPCNM0717RB

Get 2 Free Books, Plus 2 Free Gifts—

SPECIAL EXCERPT FROM

HARLEQUIN

Presents.

*Being forced to spurn Nikos Kyriazis devastated
Marnie Kenington. Years later, he offers to absolve her
family's bankruptcy—if she marries him! Nikos wants
revenge—and he knows that in the bedroom he can take
Marnie apart piece by sensual piece...*

Read on for a sneak preview of debut author
Clare Connelly's *book*
BOUGHT FOR THE BILLIONAIRE'S REVENGE.

"Now you will marry me, and he will have to spend the rest of his life knowing it was me—the man he wouldn't have in his house—who was his salvation."

The sheer fury of his words whipped Marnie like a rope. "Nikos," she said, surprised at how calm she could sound in the middle of his stormy declaration. "He should never have made you feel like that."

"Your father could have called me every name under the sun for all I cared, *agape*. It was you I expected more of."

She swallowed. Expectations were not new to Marnie. Her parents'. Her sister's. Her own.

"And now you will marry me."

Anticipation formed a cliff's edge and she was tumbling over it, free-falling from a great height. She shook her head, but they both knew it was denial for the sake of it.

"No more waiting," he intoned darkly, crushing his mouth to hers in a kiss that stole her breath and colored her soul.

His tongue clashed with hers. It was a kiss of slavish possession, a kiss designed to challenge and disarm. He blew away every defense she had, reminding her that his body had always been able to manipulate hers. A single look had always been enough to make her break out in a cold sweat of need.

"No more waiting."

"You can't still want me," she said into his mouth, wrapping her hands around his back. "You've hardly lived the life of a monk. I would have thought I'd lost all appeal by now."

"Call it unfinished business," he responded, breaking the kiss to scrape his lips down her neck, nipping at her shoulder.

She pushed her hips forward, instinctively wanting more. Wanting everything.

Her brain was wrapped in cotton wool, foggy and filled with questions softened by confusion. "It was six years ago."

"Yes. And still you're the only woman I have ever believed myself in love with. The only woman I have ever wanted a future with. Once upon a time for love."

"And now?"

"For…less noble reasons."

Don't miss
BOUGHT FOR THE BILLIONAIRE'S REVENGE,
available August 2017 wherever
Harlequin Presents® books and ebooks are sold.

www.Harlequin.com

HPEXP072017